a rhyme &
a reason

IK JAGAIT

To Mom and Dad

Chapter 1 – Me and a Girl

When you've known someone your whole life, it's hard to tell where *you* end and *they* begin. And it's hard to lose them without losing a little bit of yourself.

There was this girl I grew up with. We lived on the same street and our parents were friends, so from the time we were kids all the way through high school, we were tight. It wasn't a boyfriend-girlfriend thing, but I never felt like I needed a girlfriend because I had her. And she must have felt the same way, because she never had a boyfriend either.

In our senior year of high school, she found out she got into Stanford, which was her dream come true. She was the super smart, straight-A's, perfect SAT score type. The type you knew would end up at a fancy college before she even started kindergarten. But she was also the 'prone-to-getting-homesick' type, so Stanford, which was half an hour away from San Jose, where we lived, had always been her first and last choice.

Me, I was the total opposite. I never took school seriously and never bothered to look too far ahead. My family owned a small, but busy tandoori restaurant and I had worked there since I was a kid, so I always knew I had something to fall back on.

But when I heard about her and Stanford, it motivated me to be a little more ambitious.

A couple of my friends had gotten into Chico State, a small party school up north. It was nothing close to Stanford but it was a step above settling, and since my friends weren't too much brighter than I was, I figured if they could get in, so could I. And I was right.

For the next four years, I was at Chico and she was at Stanford. We kept in contact in the beginning, but as time went on, we just sorta lost touch for some reason. It wasn't *her* fault; she did her best to call or text every once in a while, but I was always worried about bothering her, so I didn't reach out as much. And maybe me not reaching out made her think *she* was bothering *me*, because after a while, I stopped hearing from her.

I didn't get much accomplished at Chico. Didn't even graduate. For most people, school is a way to get to where you're going, but I never had a place I was trying to go. People used to tell me I could get far if I could find a direction, and I thought college might be the place for me to do that. I was wrong. It was more like a four-year long drinking game. I had a good time and everything, but at the end I had nothing to show for it, and had to return home empty-handed.

The day I got back, her Mom was at my house. I don't remember what she was doing there, but I remember being happy to see her, because I was dreading facing my parents and knew her presence would make it easier. It wasn't that my parents were strict or demanding — they were the complete opposite. That was the problem. Letting down reasonable parents is worse than letting down *un*reasonable ones… so it was nice having someone there to soften the blow. As soon as I walked through the door, she sensed my parents' disappointment in me, and drowned it out with as much hope and optimism as she could. It didn't make them forget about paying for four years of college, but it made them feel a little less bad about it, and that was the most I could ask for.

When it was time for her to go, I walked her to the door, and thanked her for helping me out. We spent a few more minutes catching up and somewhere in the middle of that, I asked, "So what's your daughter up to?"

She got this funny look on her face. Then she smiled and said, "She's with her boyfriend."

At first, I thought she was joking. Like maybe there was someone they *referred* to as her 'boyfriend'. So I faked a laugh and said, "Wait, what? She has a boyfriend?", expecting her to say she was kidding.

She didn't. Instead she said, "Yeah, she didn't tell you?"

I said, "Nah, I haven't talked to her in a while."

Then she covered her mouth and said, "Oh, in that case maybe I shouldn't have said anything."

I guess it wasn't a joke. For a moment, I didn't know what to say. Finally, I made an attempt to play it off and said, "Damn Auntie, is that what you sent her to college to do?"

She said, "What can I say, she's outta control," and we both laughed.

She went on to tell me all about the boyfriend and how great a guy he was — how he always touched her and her husband's feet when he greeted them, how he didn't drink or smoke, how he came from a good family — but at a certain point I stopped hearing the words coming out of her mouth. I was having too much trouble trying to wrap my head around what I had just heard. It wasn't just that she had a boyfriend, it was the fact that her Mom *knew* about it. Punjabi girls don't tell their parents about their boyfriends. Mostly because, Punjabi girls aren't supposed to *have* boyfriends. And the ones that do keep it a secret for as long as they can. The only way the parents get to know is if someone finds out and tells on them, or if the relationship becomes so serious, it's time to make it official.

A couple days later, I was in my room, on the computer, looking for a new catering van for the restaurant, when the doorbell rang. My Mom answered and I heard a voice say, "Sat Sri Akal, Auntie." I recognized the voice.

My Mom responded in Punjabi, "How are you Mahi?"

It was the middle of the day but I had just gotten up and hadn't even taken a shower, so I went over to the mirrored doors on my closet to straighten myself out while they talked. Then I quickly made my bed and opened the blinds to let in a little bit of sunlight. By the time I got back to my chair, they were wrapping up their conversation. Mahi said, "Is Indo here?"

My Mom said, "Yeah, he's in his room."

We had thick carpet in our house, so you could never hear someone coming down the hallway. But I still heard every one of her footsteps in my head. My door was half open but she knocked anyway, and I turned around.

I thought she would look different. I was sure four years of college would've transformed her into someone else, but they didn't. She looked almost exactly the same — still had the same simple ponytail, the same tiny nose ring, the same hopeful eyes. Still didn't wear make-up, and still didn't need it. I was expecting to see a woman I didn't recognize, but she was still the girl I remembered.

She smiled and said, "Hey… welcome back."

I said, "Thanks."

She stood there for a moment, like she was wondering if she should walk over and give me a hug, but since I didn't stand up, she sat down on the bed instead.

I said, "Man… it's been a long time."

She said, "I know."

Anytime she hadn't seen me in a while, she would be really shy and quiet. Usually she'd wait for me to make a joke or make fun of her to break the ice, and then she'd go back to normal. But for whatever reason, I didn't do it that day, so it just stayed kinda awkward between us.

"So how was Chico?

I let out a laugh and leaned back in my chair. "It was tight. Didn't wanna come back."

"So how come you did?"

"I don't know… I was havin' too much fun. Too much fun isn't good for you."

She shrugged. "I'll take your word for it… I wouldn't know."

"Why? You didn't party it up at Stanford?"

"Not really. Mostly just studied it up."

"That sucks." My computer went to the screensaver, so I reached over and shook the mouse, then turned back to Mahi. "But hey, at least you graduated… unlike me."

She nodded. "Yeah. Oh, by the way, thanks for coming to my graduation."

"Uhh yeah, sorry about that, I just got caught up with some stuff, so—"

"It's okay, I'm just joking."

Since *I* didn't break the ice, I guess she thought *she* should give it a try. But it didn't really work and there was a long silence. And then I said, "So how's your boyfriend doing?"

As soon as she heard those words her whole demeanor changed. It was like her heart stopped beating for a moment. She said, "How did you know about that?"

I smiled and said, "I know everything."

"No, for real, who told you?"

"Look, I can't give up my sources, alright. It wouldn't be ethical."

"Was it my Mom? Did she say something when she was here?"

"Uhh, she might've mentioned it."

If Mahi was capable of getting mad, she would've been furious. But the most extreme emotion she could feel towards someone was disappointment. And she was as disappointed as I had ever seen her.

I laughed and said, "Was it supposed to be a secret or something?"

"No, it's not that… it's just… it's not that serious. We're more like friends."

She said it in a panic, but I just acted like I didn't care. I said, "What's the big deal? Nothin' wrong with having a boyfriend."

She said, "I know, but that's not what it is. She's making it sound like something it's not."

"Maybe she's just excited."

"Well there's nothing to be excited about."

"I think you might wanna tell *her* that."

"Yeah, I will."

I thought we were done with the topic, but then she stared

into my eyes and said, "I really mean it though… it's not what you think."

I knew better than to believe that. But I didn't get why she was trying so hard to convince me to.

Instead of asking her, I gave her a smile and said, "Okay… if you say so," and changed the subject. I guess I still wasn't over the idea of her having a boyfriend, so I pretended none of it mattered to me. That I was completely unaffected. I even took it so far as to act like I was happy for her.

In my mind though, I knew that even if I didn't say anything to her that day, I would say something to her eventually. When I was ready, and the time was right.

But I never got the chance. Because less than a week later, her boyfriend asked her to marry him. And she said yes.

Chapter 2 – The Wedding

Mahi's favorite game to play when we were kids was house. I think it was because she was too mature for her age and it gave her a chance to be older than she actually was. To me though, it was too 'girly' a game to get excited about, so whenever she asked me to play, I'd turn her down. But usually, after some begging and pleading, I'd give in and we'd end up playing for hours. I'd be the husband and she'd be the wife. I'd come home from work and she'd tell me all about her crazy day. Then she'd have me do yard work or fix some broken appliance, while she cooked and did the laundry. At the end, we'd put the kids, aka the stuffed animals, to bed and read them stories until they fell asleep.

She always thought I was doing her a favor by playing along, but the truth was, I didn't hate that game as much as I pretended to. There was something comforting about us being so comfortable with each other. And in a strange way, I felt even more at home in that fake house we lived in together, than in the real one I went back to when the game was over.

When I heard Mahi got engaged, I couldn't believe it. Especially after the way our conversation went. As much as she was downplaying everything, I started thinking maybe the relationship wasn't as serious as I first thought. But it turned out to be more serious than I ever could've imagined.

The wedding date was set for December of that year, about six months after he proposed, and during those six months, I avoided her completely. I started working long hours at the restaurant to keep myself busy, while secretly believing the wedding wouldn't take place. It didn't make sense to me that it would. I knew something would go wrong and put an end to it. It had to. So, I just waited for that something to happen.

A month went by, and then another month and then another, and it was all still going according to plan. Every once in a while, I'd get updates about the progress — a reception venue being booked in Fremont, a maroon color theme being chosen for the bride's side, a foreign relative getting their visa approved so they could attend the wedding — and with each piece of news, it became harder for me to stay in denial.

Before I knew it, it was the week of the wedding, and finally it hit me that this miracle I was waiting for wasn't coming. And not only was this wedding gonna take place, *I* was gonna have to *attend* it. Now, the best I could hope for was a way out.

A Punjabi wedding isn't a ceremony that lasts a couple hours; it's a festival that lasts a whole week. Every day there's a different ritual to perform and each one's a bigger deal than the last. In the mornings, I would drive by her house on my way to work and I could feel the momentum building — more guests, more decorations, more excitement. I steered clear of it all for the most part, but I knew I could only avoid it for so long.

The night before the wedding is the Jaago, the biggest pre-wedding event. It's like a mini reception — there's singing, dancing and drinking, and it ends with a giant parade through the neighborhood. In Punjab, the parade was a way to invite the neighbors to the wedding and it was a common occurrence, so everyone knew what was going on. But when they first brought the tradition to America, it usually ended up with the cops being called. A hundred brown people unexpectedly marching down the street in the middle of the night would freak people out. Eventually though, families wised up and started giving out warnings in advance, and nowadays, the neighbors will sometimes even join in on the celebration.

If I didn't show up to the Jaago, it would've raised some eyebrows for sure, so I didn't have much of a choice but to go. The only thing in my control was the amount of time I had to stay, and I did whatever I could to minimize it. I came home late from the restaurant, took my time getting ready, and started thinking of excuses I could give for having to leave early. When I was finally good to go, I took a deep breath and walked out of the house.

She lived four houses down, on the opposite side of the street, and I remember hoping to get hit by a car on my way there.

By the time I arrived, the party was in full swing and I could feel the house vibrating. Judging by how many cars were parked outside, there had to be at least a hundred people in there and a good portion of them knew who I was. Mahi's relatives treated me like family and mine treated her the same way, so I couldn't really be inconspicuous.

In the front yard there was a big, bright tent set up where all the uncles were drinking whiskey, eating goat and having a loud debate about something only they could understand. I walked through the tent, greeting the ones I recognized and acknowledging the ones I didn't, then made my way into the house.

Regardless of how I was feeling, I couldn't help but be overwhelmed by the atmosphere. A Punjabi wedding house is a sight to behold. There was colorful fabric draped on the walls, bright lights hanging from the ceiling, flower vines wrapped around the windows and doorways, and people dressed in fancy kurtas and lehengas. For a moment, the warmth and beauty of it all transcended the ugliness inside me.

My destination was the backyard. I knew that's where all the young guys would be hanging out, and it was the best place for me to ride this thing out. But to get there I had to pass through the living room, where most of the crowd was gathered.

Everyone was so caught up in the festivities that I was able to blend in, and for a moment, I thought I would go unnoticed. But as I made my way through, I started to get recognized. "Oh wow, haven't seen you in a while." "Hey Indo, where you been?" "So when are *you* getting married?" "You know you're next in line, right?" I responded to each of them as politely as I could while continuing to push forward. My eyes were looking straight ahead and I tried my hardest to keep'em focused in that direction... but at a certain point, I couldn't help myself.

Mahi was sitting on the floor, decked out from head to toe. I had known her my whole life, so it should have been odd seeing her looking like that. But it wasn't. Not even a little. Everything, from her outfit, to her jewelry, to the mehndi on her hands seemed like it belonged on her. Almost as if the idea of a bride was created with *her* in mind.

She was surrounded by family and friends and they were

singing old wedding folk songs. I don't think I've ever seen a group of people more happy. Especially her Mom and Dad. For Punjabi parents, your kid's wedding is like your Super Bowl. It's the moment you're waiting for since the day they're born. But if it's your daughter's wedding, the moment's bittersweet because it marks the end of her time with you. And soon enough, the scene in front of me went from sweet to bitter. One of the older women in the crowd broke out into a song about a daughter leaving her parents' home and everyone started to tear up. I looked around at all the emotional faces and suddenly got this feeling that I was intruding. That I was somehow contaminating the sincerity of their feelings. So, I got out of there as quickly as I could.

As soon as I stepped outside, I heard a voice say, "This motherfucker finally decides to show up!" It was Paul, Mahi's older brother.

Paul was a guy that I looked up to while growing up. He was this big, brash dude who was known as the 'bad boy' of his family. But even though younger kids like me admired that reputation, he himself hated it. It was almost like a trigger for him. Whenever it was mentioned, it would set him off. Paul was good at heart, but he had two destructive qualities: a bad temper and a love of alcohol. And the more alcohol he drank, the worse his temper got. Once I saw how drunk he was, I knew he was the answer to my problems.

He called me over to a table set up underneath the string light wrapped apricot tree in the middle of their yard. I walked down the brick pathway through the grass and joined them just as they were about to do shots. Paul looked at his cousin, who was pouring, and said "Pour another one."

I said, "Nah, I'm good man."

He looked at me like he didn't wanna hear it. Then he turned back to the cousin and said, "Go ahead."

"No, seriously bro, I don't want one."

"Shut the fuck up — you don't have a choice."

He wasn't taking no for an answer. And every time he insisted, I resisted. And the more I resisted, the angrier he got. Our back-and-forth escalated, and the other guys started to feel the tension. They were looking at each other like they were wondering if this was something they could laugh off or needed to get involved in.

Then Paul got a step closer to me and said, "You don't show up all week, and now, when you finally do, you don't wanna drink with us?"

I just shrugged and gave him a blank stare, which to him was worse than a slap in the face. He shook his head and said, "Man, you used to be the homie. I don't know what happened to you in Chico, but you came back a little bitch."

If there were any questions about the seriousness of our argument, they went out the window. A few of the others finally spoke up and made some half-assed attempts to keep the peace. But peace wasn't what I was looking for. I looked straight ahead, away from Paul, and under my breath said, "I'd rather be a bitch than my family's fuck-up."

Everyone fell silent. We were past the point of no return, and now, the most they could do was break up the fight that was gonna start at any moment. I braced myself for whatever Paul was gonna throw at me — a slap across my face, a punch in the stomach, or if I was lucky, maybe just a hard push to the ground.

It turned out to be none of the above. He put me in a head

lock. But not the kind you try to hurt someone with. He laughed and said, "I missed your smart-ass mouth, fucker. Welcome back."

I couldn't believe it. Everyone in that backyard, including me, was sure I was about to get knocked out. But Paul's one and only sister was getting married and that was something he wasn't gonna ruin. He let go of the headlock, put his hands together and said, "Now please, take a fuckin' shot with us."

I didn't know what to say.

"Are you gonna make me beg you?"

Then he bent down to touch my feet. At that point, there was only one thing left for me to do. I looked around at everyone, then back at Paul, and said, "Pour the fuckin' shot." Everyone let out a celebratory cheer, and before I knew it, I was marching down the street in the back of the Jaago parade.

I gave in. I drank when they told me to drink. I danced when they told me to dance. I smiled when they told me to smile. The only thing I wouldn't do was look at Mahi. As long as I didn't see her, I could at least try to forget what I was celebrating.

Having to be at the Jaago was one thing, but going to the wedding was something else altogether. That was where I drew the line. The next morning, I went to my last resort: faking sick. Between the hangover and my state of mind, it wasn't a tough act to pull off.

My Dad came into my room, tying his tie, and found me still in bed. He asked me what was going on and when I told him, he thought I was joking. "Stop messing around and get ready."

I said, "I can't."

"What do you mean you can't? We're getting late!"

Then my Mom showed up. "You're still not up?"

My Dad filled her in. "He said he's not going. He doesn't feel good."

She couldn't believe it. "This is *Mahi's* wedding. How can you not go? What are we gonna tell everyone?"

They both tried their hardest to convince me, but my mind was made up, and eventually they had no choice but to give up and leave without me.

I spent all day alone at the house, still holding out hope that my miracle might happen. Passing the time was the hardest part. I tried eating, but wasn't hungry; I tried watching TV, but couldn't pay attention; I tried sleeping, but my eyes wouldn't stay closed. Every time I looked at the clock, I couldn't stop myself from picturing what must have been going on at the Gurdwara at that time. Finally, at some point in the late afternoon while I was sitting in my room, I heard the front door open and my parents walking in. They were talking. But they weren't talking about the crazy thing that happened at the wedding and how it put a stop to everything. They were talking about the most random thing — some work around the house that needed to be done.

That was when I realized it was all over. Mahi was married.

Chapter 3 – Saturday Night

A few months before the wedding, Mahi's husband got a job at a hedge fund in Sacramento, so as soon they got married, they moved away.

For the next couple years, my life was about two things and two things only — working and going out. Weekdays at the restaurant; weekends at the club. When you're a kid, you can't wait for school to end so you can go play. When you're an adult, the story doesn't really change. You just outgrow one playground and grow *into* another.

But no matter how much time passed or how much I partied or how many different girls I got involved with, I couldn't completely get over what happened. And why it happened. And how it happened. I thought that eventually the memory of it all would fade away... but it never did.

One night in February, we were out in downtown San Jose. It was a typical Saturday night. There were usually about 4 or 5 of us — me and my cousin Lucky were the two regulars, and the others were always alternating. That night, it was Marcus and Domingo. If you asked someone to describe San Jose nightlife, they'd probably use words like 'grimy' or 'ghetto', but that was exactly what we liked about it. There was a rawness to that place. The guys there were a little more aggressive and the girls were a little more wild. The atmosphere was dangerous but you were never really in any danger, and that brought everyone together in a way that a more upscale city never could. San Jose wasn't for everyone, but it was just the place for us.

We had a routine whenever we went out. First, we'd pick up a bottle of Crown from the liquor store and some sodas from McDonald's or Jack-in-the-Box. Then we'd drive downtown and drink in the parking lot. Once we were good and faded, we'd head to the club. Most people buy drinks at the bar, but that never really made any sense to us. *Our* method wasn't exactly legal, but it was a lot more fiscally responsible.

That night, we were in an underground parking lot on San Fernando, drinking in Lucky's Mustang and having a good time, when I turned to my right and saw this beautiful girl staring at me through the window. She had highlighted, golden brown hair and these mischievous eyes that looked like they could see right through me. I stared back at her for a moment, mesmerized. Then, I gave her my smoothest smile. But she didn't smile back. Instead, she started fixing her hair. That's when I realized she wasn't looking at *me*; she was looking at her reflection. Our windows were tinted, so she had no idea anybody was even in the car.

As soon as Lucky noticed her, he looked at me, then immediately pressed down on the window button which made her jump backwards. We made eye contact for a second, then she smiled and said, "Oh shit, my bad", and ran off to catch up with her friends. Lucky yelled, "Yo! Where you going?" as she disappeared out of sight.

The walk from the parking lot to the club was always one of the best parts of the night. As we passed around the Jack-in-the-Box cup and took our final sips, the drunkenness would peak and Lucky would start hitting on every girl that walked by. If you're gonna go out, you want someone in your group who has no shame whatsoever. Someone who can take rejection like a champ and keep coming back for more. Those crazy, unpredictable friends are the ones that make going out worthwhile and memorable, and for us, Lucky was that guy.

As we were getting in line at the club, Lucky was loudly telling us about a wedding in Canada he had just gotten back from. He was talking about the girls out there and said something along the lines of, "They got so many bad bitches." He had barely finished the sentence when this blonde girl standing in front of us in line turned around, clearly unhappy with Lucky's choice of words, and said, "Seriously?" We were all a little surprised. Then her friends turned around too.

It's weird. With some people you come across, you just get this sense that they're a part of your story. Or that *you're* a part of *theirs*. When I saw that girl in the parking lot, for some reason I knew I'd be seeing her again, and sure enough, one of this angry blonde's friends was her. We gave each other a look, acknowledging our previous encounter as the angry blonde continued, "Did you really just refer to women as bitches?"

Lucky said, "Uhhh yeah… but this was kind of a private conversation."

She said, "Well you're in PUBLIC, in case you didn't notice."

"Okay well, I'll try to keep my voice down then."

"That's not the point!"

"What *is* the point?"

"The fact that you don't *know* the point, is the point."

"Okay now you're just confusing me."

We all cracked up, and even the parking lot girl couldn't help but let out a laugh. The angry blonde immediately turned to her and said, "Really? You think this is funny?"

The parking lot girl tried to put on a straight face.

"What? No... I was... laughing about something else."

The angry blonde shook her head. "You know what, whatever."

The parking lot girl put her arms around the blonde. "Aww come on, don't be like that."

"See this is why women can never get anywhere... cause we don't support each other."

"Oh my god, I *am* supporting you."

"How? By laughing at me?"

"Are you for real right now? You're really gonna let some random assholes turn you against me?"

I did my best impression of the angry blonde and said, "Seriously? Did you really just refer to men as assholes?"

She gave me a playful smile and said, "Shut up!"

We reached the front of the line and they turned around to hand their IDs to the bouncer. As he was looking them over, the angry blonde leaned towards him, pointed at us and whispered something into his ear. The bouncer listened, took a long look at us, then said, "I'm sorry guys, you gotta go somewhere else."

We couldn't believe it. As she entered the club, the angry blonde made sure to look back and taunt us. What a dick. In one stroke, she got us barred from the club and put an end to my budding romance with the parking lot girl. Before she disappeared into the club, the parking lot girl looked back at me one last time. Most girls don't want you to know they're into you, but some like to make it obvious. Almost like they're daring you to do something about it.

We pleaded our case to the bouncer, but it was no use. Bouncers are either cheerful, friendly guys who want you to have a good time, or uptight dudes who think they're guarding a government building. This guy was one of the latter. We had no choice but to move on.

Clubs, in general, get a bad rap. They're looked at as places where sleazy, shallow people do sleazy, shallow things. There's some of that going on for sure, but for the most part, the reputation's undeserved. And it was probably given by people who never figured out how to be comfortable in a club, so they judged those who did. Don't get me wrong, ugly things do happen. Wherever there's alcohol involved, that's inevitable. But if you can learn to become one with the raw, reckless energy of a club, beautiful things can happen too.

Later on in the night, we were at Loft, an always-packed, two-level club on 2nd Street. Loft was the type of place you never made *plans* for, but would always find yourself in by the end of the night. All the other spots gave you some sort of obstacle to overcome — a cover, a dress code, a dick bouncer — but Loft welcomed everyone with open arms. You'd go in with no expectations, but always come out with a story to tell.

Me and Domingo were on the packed dance floor and Lucky and Marcus were at the bar. As we were scoping out the scene, I looked across the sea of people and saw the parking lot girl, dancing with one of her friends. At that point I was pretty intoxicated, so I wasn't sure if she was really there or I was imagining things. I turned away from her, waited for a few minutes, then turned back around. She was still there, except this time I could swear she was a little closer. Over the next few songs, the distance between us slowly disappeared and before I knew it, we were back to back. Then, she started 'accidentally' bumping into me. I took the hint and turned around.

The moment a girl backs up into you on the dance floor is the moment the night is officially considered a success. Until that happens, you're wandering around with a nagging feeling of incompleteness. But once it does, it's like you're made whole again.

After a few minutes of grinding, she spun around and we stared into each other's eyes, both drunk out of our minds. I slowly leaned forward, wondering if she'd pull back. She didn't. Instead, she closed her eyes. But just as our lips were about to touch… her friend pulled her away.

There's always a cock-blocking, hater friend around to ruin a beautiful moment. I got ready to call her out, but before I could open my mouth, she pointed to some commotion at the bar, where it looked like a fight had broken out. As the scene came into focus, I saw that Lucky and the angry blonde were in the middle of it all. Shit. What the hell did he get himself into now? I forgot to mention the downside of those 'crazy and unpredictable' friends — they get into trouble. And when they do, *you* usually have to bail them out.

As we pushed our way through the crowd, I lost sight of Lucky, until I saw two bouncers dragging him away. Me and Domingo rushed over and I tapped one of them on the shoulder. But when he turned around, I realized it wasn't Lucky they were dragging away, it was some other guy with the same color shirt. We looked back at the bar and saw Lucky standing there with a drink in his hand and a smirk on his face. Nothing made any sense, so we went over and asked him what happened.

Apparently, him and Marcus were at the bar when the angry blonde showed up. They gave each other a few dirty looks, then went about their business. A few moments later, this 'Rico Suave' type dude pulled up and started hitting on the angry blonde. She was kinda diggin' him, so they started talking and having a good time, but somewhere in the middle of their conversation, he slipped something into her drink. No one noticed except Lucky. Just as she was about to take a sip, Lucky knocked the drink out of her hand and all hell broke loose. She started yelling at him and the bartender called the bouncers, who showed up ready to kick Lucky out. He told them what happened, but no one believed him. After some begging and pleading, he finally convinced them to check Rico Suave's pockets. At first, Rico Suave acted innocent and casually reached into his pockets like he had nothing to hide. But all of a sudden, he tried to make a run for it and the bouncers pounced on him. The angry blonde's jaw dropped, and Lucky kindly picked it up off the floor.

When the night was over, we'd always head to La Vic's Taqueria, which was the place to be after the clubs closed down. It was the unofficial after-party. They'd have a long line going out the door, loud music playing, and people dancing while they waited for their food.

Our group and the angry blonde's group sat at the same table. Since Lucky had saved her life, we were all friends now. Me and the parking lot girl were sitting across from each other, and after another round of sneaky eye contact, I got up, walked over and sat down next to her. She smiled without looking at me and started acting shy. I say 'acting' because it was obvious she wasn't the shy type. She had this playful demeanor that was impossible to hide. I said, "What was your name again?"

She said, "I never told you my name."

"Why not?"

"Because you never asked."

I said, "Oh," and there was a long silence.

She said, "Well... are you gonna ask?"

That was when one of her friends, a petite but tough-looking Filipino chick, got annoyed by all the cutesiness and said, "Her name is Jasleen!"

I laughed, but the friend wasn't finished. "Do you want her phone number?"

The parking lot girl, or Jasleen, objected, "Hey, what the hell?"

The friend said, "Bitch, don't even," and proceeded to give me the number.

It's funny, the difference between guys and girls when going out. A guy's mission is to get something before the end of the night; a girl's is to not lose anything. Usually, if one succeeds it means the other one fails, but Jasleen's friend made it so that we both got what we wanted.

Chapter 4 – A Pretty Soul

For the next few days, me and Jasleen were texting and calling each other, and I learned some things about her. She was twenty-one, a business student at San Jose State, and it turned out she was Punjabi. Which wasn't a good thing or a bad thing — it was just a thing. If someone's the same race as you, it's a thing.

I also found out she had just gotten out of a bad, four-year-long relationship. It all started out normal, but the longer they were together, the more controlling her boyfriend became. He started telling her what to wear and what not to wear. He made it so that he could track her location at all times, and if she was in a place he didn't recognize, he'd blow up her phone and demand an explanation. Any time she didn't answer a call or a text right away, he'd become suspicious and accuse her of cheating. He even got into fights with her male friends because he was convinced there was 'something going on' and once got into it with one of her *cousins* for the same reason.

Whenever Jasleen took a stand and tried to break up with him, he'd cause a bunch of drama and make vague suicide threats that would scare her into sticking together. Then things would get better for a while, and he'd turn back into the charming guy he was when they first met. But as soon as she'd get comfortable again, he'd fall right back into the same pattern. This cycle went on for years. Jasleen said the crazy thing was, she used to talk shit about girls who were in these kinds of relationships, and then somehow, became one herself.

One day, they were having another one of their heated arguments and he got so angry, he hit her. It was the first time he had ever done that and he immediately regretted it, but Jasleen got this feeling deep down that it wouldn't be the last. So she finally worked up the courage to break free for good and made up her mind that no matter how hard he tried, she would resist his attempts to get her back. He used everything from apologies and promises to threats and emotional blackmail, but nothing worked. Jasleen held firm, and eventually, he gave up. The last time she heard from him was two weeks before we met.

Like a lot of other girls, Jasleen called her ex-boyfriend 'over-protective', which always sounded like a generous term to me. I can understand a parent being over-protective of their child, or maybe a brother being over-protective of his sister, but a boyfriend being over-protective of his girlfriend? What exactly is he protecting her from? I know there are some sick dudes out there who can do some messed up things, but is *that* who he's really worried about? When he's sitting at home and she's out there on her own, is he afraid that she'll be *attacked* by someone… or is he more concerned that she'll be *attracted* to someone? Someone other than him. And are all his attempts to control her just a way to avoid how bad that would make him feel. If that's the case, then I guess "over-protective" *is* the right term, except it isn't his girlfriend he's trying to protect, it's himself.

After getting to know each other a little bit, I brought up the idea of seeing each other again. She agreed, and I told her to meet me at this movie theater parking lot, which was my go-to spot for first dates.

We both got there around the same time and stood by our cars for a moment, looking at each other from a distance. She was sipping on a large Taco Bell drink. I said, "What's in the cup?"

She said, "Vodka. You want some?"

I put out my hand.

She faked an evil laugh and said, "Just kidding. It's sprite."

I smiled and put down my hand.

We were both quiet for a little bit, then she asked, "So, are we gonna watch a movie or…?"

I said, "We *can*… or we can just talk."

"Why? Your mom forgot to give you ticket money?"

I laughed. "No. I forgot to ask her."

She looked around the parking lot. "So where are we gonna talk?"

I turned around, looked at the backseat of my Acura, then looked back at her.

She said, "Uhh… yeah, I don't know about all that."

It probably came across as a little crude, but to me there was no place more romantic. Somewhere a guy and a girl could shut out the rest of the world and get to know each other without the pretense of dinner or a movie.

I said, "You sure? It's nice and warm in there."

It was one of those cold Bay Area spring evenings and I could tell she was freezing. She tried to tough it out but finally gave in. "Okay, but we're just gonna TALK."

"Of course. What else would we do?"

I got into the backseat and slid over to make room for her… but she pulled a fast one and sat in the front. I said, "I was thinking back *here*."

She said, "I'm sure you were."

We were both quiet for a bit and then she said, "So… tell me something about yourself."

"What do you wanna know?"

She thought about it. "Do you have a girlfriend?"

She had asked me that question while we were texting, but I didn't give her a clear answer.

I said, "I already told you… I got a few."

"Okay, so you're like… a player?"

"I wouldn't say that. I'm just a friendly guy."

She laughed. "Okay, Mr. Friendly Guy. If you have so many girlfriends, what are you doing here with me? Are you trying to add me to your collection?"

I pretended to be offended. "Or maybe I just wanted to get to know you."

She wasn't buying it.

I said, "So you gonna come back here or what?

She said, "No", and took a sip of her drink.

"Why not? You don't trust yourself?"

She almost spit out the Sprite. "Trust *myself?!* More like, I don't trust YOU."

"If you didn't trust me, you wouldn't have got into my car in the first place."

She didn't have an answer, so I continued, "But it's cool though. If you don't think you'd be able to keep your hands off me, then maybe you *should* stay up there. It's probably for the best."

She gave me a long, blank stare, then suddenly started crawling into the backseat. I knew she was too smart to fall for reverse psychology, but I guess she didn't think *I* was smart

27

enough to realize that about her. Whatever the case, I wasn't complaining. She pulled down the cup holder to create a divider between us, then sat as far away from me as possible and said, "Happy?"

I said, "I'm happy if you're happy."

She kicked me in the leg. As I winced in pain, she said, "So let's talk about your girlfriends, shall we?"

"Do we have to?"

"Why… is it a touchy subject for you?"

"No."

"Okay then."

"So what about'em?"

"Who are they?"

"They're girls… that are friends."

"What do you do with them?"

"Stuff."

"What kinda stuff?"

"Stuff."

"Do you have S-E-X with them?"

"Only if they're nice to me."

"I'm serious."

"Me too."

She sighed in frustration. "Okay look… I'm gonna ask you the same question, and this time I want a real answer. If you have all these girlfriends, like you claim, what do you want from *me*?"

Now, it was time to give her my speech. The speech I gave every girl I got involved with. I put my hands in the pockets of my jacket, leaned back against the door and said, "Look, me and you can do whatever you wanna do… and we can *not* do

28

whatever you *don't* wanna do. But if you're looking for a boy-friend... that's not me. Because nothing that happens between us is gonna stop me from seeing other girls. So if you're okay with that, cool. But if you're not okay with it... that's cool too."

She reacted to the speech the way most girls did — with disappointment. She said, "Okay, well... I'm not really that type of girl, so..."

But just like the other girls, the disappointment wasn't strong enough for her to walk away. She stuck around. They all did for at least a little while — some for a few days, some for a few weeks, some a few months. Sooner or later though, they realized this arrangement wasn't for them. The only question now was, how long would *Jasleen* last?

Before things became too awkward, I changed the subject, and she slowly returned to her playful mood. And as we talked about one random thing after another, I lifted up the cup holder and inched closer and closer to her, until I was as close as I could get. Just like in the club, we stared deeply into each other's eyes. And just like in the club... we were interrupted.

There was a knock on the window. A cop was standing there, staring down at us. Jasleen freaked out, and I backed away from her and rolled down the window. The cop pointed a flash-light in our faces and said, "What's going on guys?

I said, "Nothing. Just hangin' out."

"Really? This is an interesting place to hang out."

"Yeah, well... we're interesting people."

The cop didn't appreciate my attitude, and neither did Jasleen. She gave me a hard nudge in the stomach. The cop said, "Is that right?"

I looked at him and shrugged. We hadn't done anything, so

I wasn't worried, but Jasleen was acting like we got caught with our clothes off. At the drop of a hat, she went from bad-ass chick to scared little girl.

The cop gave us each a long stare, then said, "Maybe find a better place to hang out."

He got back in his car and sat there, waiting for us to leave. Jasleen breathed a sigh of relief and decided it'd be best to quit while we were ahead. She said, "I should probably get going."

I said, "You sure? We can just go somewhere else."

"Nah, I don't wanna take any chances."

I could tell she was a little spooked, so I didn't wanna push it. "Alright, that's cool."

On her way home, she called me and we laughed about the entire incident. And even though our first 'date' had a premature ending, it really felt like it was the beginning of something special.

* * *

For the next couple days, I didn't hear from Jasleen, which was weird because she had been texting me at least a couple times a day since the night we met. I told myself she was probably busy with school and left it alone for a while, but finally I decided to text her myself. No response. The next day I tried again. Still no response. I started thinking about what happened in the car that night, wondering if I had said or done something wrong, but no matter how many times I went over it in my head, nothing stood out. I let another day or two pass and tried calling her. No answer; no call back. It was strange. The only thing I could think of was that she gave more thought to my 'speech' and decided it wasn't something she wanted to get involved in. Eventually, I accepted that explanation and made up my mind to move on. But I was disappointed. More disappointed than I thought I would be. This was the first girl since Mahi I actually felt something for. Pretty faces are everywhere, but a pretty soul is hard to find, and it didn't feel good to let another one slip away.

The following Wednesday was St. Patrick's Day, and we were set to go out again. Lucky's parents were out of town, so we were pre-gaming at his house. Regardless of how long they were gone for, parents being out of the house was always something you took full advantage of, so Lucky had brought out his Dad's best liquor bottles and lined them up on the kitchen island where we were all drinking. Most of them were just for show though, since none of us really liked to venture beyond Crown or Remy.

Lucky was a gun nut, and anytime we were at his house, he liked to show off his latest toys. That night, he was telling us all about a new pistol he had just bought. "What's sick about 1911s is you can carry'em cocked and locked."

Marcus, like the rest of us, wasn't really interested or impressed. "That's real fascinating bro… now can you put that shit away before you kill someone?"

Lucky said, "Chill out, it's not even loaded."

"Yeah that's usually the last thing you hear before getting accidentally shot in the face."

"Oh my god. Look I'll show you."

As he was attempting to show us, the gun got pointed in

Domingo's direction. "Woah, woah! Don't point that shit at me!"

Lucky said, "Jesus bro. Y'all watch too many movies."

"Just put it away man, you're killin' everyone's buzz."

"Fine... fuck."

Lucky took the gun into his bedroom, shaking his head in disappointment. "I need to get some white friends, I swear."

Domingo said, "What you talkin' about? I'm half white."

Lucky came back out of the room. "Yeah but your first name is *two and a half* Mexican."

We all laughed. As Lucky sat back down, Marcus said, "Don't worry, we'll help you find some white friends tonight."

"Find me some white *bitches* and I'll be even happier."

"What, like that one from last time?"

Lucky tilted his head back. "Oh man, don't remind me of her. I saved her fuckin' life and she still wouldn't give up the number." Then he looked at me and said, "Hey what happened with that one *you* were talking to?"

I said, "I don't know. We chilled one time, then she kinda just disappeared on me."

"Well, hit her up."

"Why?"

"Tell her to come through and bring her friends. I mean, not the white one, but... I'm sure she got some other bad ones."

"I haven't heard from her in like 2 weeks."

"Just call'er real quick."

"I already did. She never called me back."

"Try again."

"Bro it's no use."

"Man, stop being a pussy."

I rolled my eyes.

"Or give *me* the number. *I'll* call'er."

Even though he wasn't admitting it, the real reason Lucky wanted me to call was the angry blonde. He was still stuck on her and wanted another chance with her through Jasleen.

So he kept pushing me, and finally I was like, "Okay, fine." I took out my phone, dialed, and put it on speaker. It rang and rang and I looked at Lucky and said, "See?" But just as I was about to hang up, Jasleen answered.

I took the phone off speaker and said, "Hey, what's up?" as I went into the other room.

She said, "Nothing."

Something was wrong; I could hear it in her voice. We had an awkward, stilted conversation for a minute or so and then out of nowhere she said, "Can you come meet me?"

We were just about ready to go. The buzz was kicking in and the Uber was on its way... but I couldn't say no.

As soon as I came out of the room, Lucky was eager to know what happened. "Is she comin' through?"

I said, "Uhh, nah... but hey, I'll catch up with y'all in a bit. I'm gonna go see her real quick."

They immediately started giving me shit. Lucky said, "Seriously? You're gonna abandon your boys for some *chick*?"

"Motherfucker, *you* were the one who told me to call her."

"Yeah, so her and her friends could come out with us, not so you could go on a fuckin' date."

"It ain't a date, it's just gonna be a quick little thing. I'll meet you guys there."

"You better, bitch. It's St. Patrick's Day."

I grabbed my things and took off to her school, which was

where she wanted to meet. She didn't tell me what was going on, but I had a feeling it had something to do with her ex-boyfriend. I remembered her saying she couldn't believe he finally decided to leave her alone. That it almost felt 'too good to be true'. Maybe it was.

When I got there, I saw her sitting alone, wearing a thick winter parka, on a bench outside the campus. She looked like a completely different person from the one I remembered. Her hair was a mess and her face seemed worn down. It had only been two weeks but it seemed like years had passed. All the life and energy she was filled with had been sucked out. I got out of the car, walked up to her and said, "Yo... what's going on?"

She said, "Hey, uhh... nothing", without looking me in the eyes.

"You okay?"

"Yeah... I'm fine."

She was doing everything in her power to keep from falling apart. But I got the sense it was only a matter of time.

I said, "You sure? You don't look fine."

"No, yeah... I just... wanted to see you."

"Really? How come?"

She didn't respond.

"Did something happen?"

She was still facing away, but I could see her eyes start to well up.

"Jasleen... what's wrong?"

Finally, she looked up at me and said, "I'm pregnant."

I was right; it *did* have something to do with her ex-boyfriend. Just not in the way I thought.

I let out a heavy breath and said, "Fuck." Then, as carefully

34

as possible, I asked, "So... the father... it's..."

She nodded.

I shook my head and sat down next to her on the bench. "So... what are you gonna do?"

She said, "You know how hard it was to get away from him? I'm not going back. There's no way I'm gonna do that."

"Okay... then..."

"I'm not keeping it. I have an appointment tomorrow morning."

It made sense. All things considered, she didn't really have any other option. But I still didn't understand what she wanted from *me*.

She turned to me and said, "Look, I haven't told anybody about this. Like no one at all. And I don't plan to. But they said I can't drive after the... procedure is done." She paused for a moment, then hesitantly asked, "Do you think you can drop me off and pick me up once it's over?"

She made it sound like all she needed was a ride, but it felt like it was more than that. Like she was scared and didn't wanna go through it alone. I could understand that, but I was still surprised she asked me of all people. Maybe it was because I was someone completely outside of her world, so there was no danger of anyone she knew finding out. I took a moment to let everything sink in, then said, "Yeah, of course."

She said, "I mean, I know it's a lot to ask, so if you're busy, it's totally fine. I can just Uber it or something."

"No, no, I'm free. Just let me know when and where and I'll be there."

"Are you sure?"

"Yeah."

35

"Okay… thank you. I gotta get going, my Mom's blowing up my phone, but my appointment's at 8 in the morning, so if you can just meet me here around 7… that would be good."

I nodded. "I'll see you then."

She stood up and said, "Thank you so much." Then she started looking me up and down. A few seconds later, she reached over and pinched me on the arm.

I said, "What was that?"

She said, "You're not wearing green." And she walked away.

I felt my phone vibrate. It was a text from Lucky asking how much longer I would be. A club was the last place I wanted to be at that point, so I told'em I wasn't gonna make it, and headed home. I knew they'd give me a hard time the next time I saw them, but I was just gonna have to put up with it.

It was the weirdest thing. Jasleen had dropped this huge news on me, but for the rest of that night, the only thing I could think about was that pinch on my arm.

Chapter 5 – Far From Okay

In my sophomore year of college, my friend Thomas's Dad was killed by a drunk driver while riding his bike. It was one of those freak things where if he would've left the house a second earlier, or a second later, nothing would've happened. Obviously, Thomas was devastated and I wanted to do what I could to help him get through it, but I felt like I should do more than just the bare minimum. More than just 'being there' for him. So, I tried to put myself in his shoes and imagine what it would be like if it was *my* Dad who was killed by that drunk driver. What would be going on in my head? What would I want from everyone around me? And what, if anything, would make it hurt a little less?

Doing that helped me figure out what to say and what not to say. When to be with him, and when to give him space. When to hold him together, and when to let him fall apart. I don't know if I made that experience any easier for Thomas, but I at least understood the nightmare he was going through.

But there are some shoes you can't put yourself in, no matter how hard you try. They just don't fit. What does it mean to have a baby growing inside of you? And what does it feel like when it's not there anymore?

I got to her school just before sunrise, and Jasleen was sitting in her car with the engine still running — probably for the heater. She was one of those girls who got cold very easily. I pulled up right next to her, but she didn't even notice me for a while. Finally, she turned and looked, and quickly got into my car.

The clinic was in Gilroy, about 30 minutes away, and the drive there was quiet. After thanking me again, Jasleen barely said another word. I didn't really know what to say to her either. I asked her if she was okay, but all she did was shrug. Maybe it was a stupid question, because she was about as far from 'okay' as someone could be.

Once we entered the parking lot, she said, "You can just drop me off here."

I felt kinda weird about that, so I said, "Nah, I'll come inside."

I'd always wondered what an abortion clinic looked like. I would have been perfectly okay with never finding out, but a part of me was curious. For whatever reason, I thought it would be some dimly lit, run-down, depressing place but it turned out to be just like any other doctor's office I'd ever been to. Obviously the experience was a little different because of the circumstances, but the place itself was surprisingly comforting.

The lady at the front desk greeted us warmly, had Jasleen fill out some paperwork, and told us to have a seat. There were two other girls in the waiting room, and judging by the looks on their faces, they were there for the same reason as us. The only difference was they were both alone, which made me glad I decided to come inside. I don't know what it's like to be in that position, but I imagine it doesn't make it any easier being in it by yourself.

The entire time we were waiting, I was thinking about whether or not I should give Jasleen a hug before they took her in. It was a weird thing to be fixated on, but that was the only thought circling around in my head. The situation was so delicate, I didn't wanna do the wrong thing. I kept peaking at her from the corner of my eye, hoping she would break down, so that I could give her the support I thought she needed. But she was stone-faced. And it made me realize that I wasn't the only one who didn't understand what she was feeling. Neither did she.

Finally, a nurse came out and called Jasleen's name. We both stood up and I turned to her, still unsure about what to do. Do I hug her or not? I decided I'd wait for her to look at me, and maybe her eyes would give me the answer. But they didn't need to, because before I could do anything, *she* hugged *me*.

After letting go, she followed the nurse to the back. But I could still feel her arms around me long after she was gone. I felt them on my way out of the clinic, as I walked through the parking lot, and as I got back in my car. And for some reason, I couldn't bring myself to drive away. Even though it didn't make any sense, I felt like I'd be abandoning her if I took off. So I just sat there for the longest time.

It must have been at least half an hour before I snapped out of the spell I was under and decided I should go. I put the key in the ignition, but I didn't even get to turn it, because my phone started to vibrate. It was Jasleen. It was supposed to take 3 or 4 hours so it was strange that she was calling. I picked up and said, "Hello?"

"Are you far away?

"Nah, I'm still here."

"Okay, I'll be out in a second."

She hung up without an explanation. I drove to the front and got there just as she was walking out. She got into the car, looking even more distraught than before.

I said, "What happened?"

She started to cry. I didn't wanna press her for an answer, so I just waited for her to tell me something. Finally, she turned to me with tears in her eyes and said, "I couldn't do it."

I didn't know what to say. "Uhh, okay... that's okay. Umm, so... what... do you wanna do?"

"I don't know... let's just get outta here."

"Alright, yeah."

I ended up taking her to a quiet hilltop overlooking the city, where me and Lucky would sometimes go to smoke weed. It was a good place to get away from the rest of the world and talk. And there was definitely a lot to talk about.

This was more or less the end of Jasleen's life. She was an unmarried, pregnant Punjabi girl who couldn't bring herself to get an abortion or tell anybody who the father of her baby was. As much as I wanted to tell her that everything would be alright, I couldn't. Because it wouldn't.

She said, "I'm sorry I wasted your time."

I said, "It's okay. I've never been to an abortion clinic before, so I can cross that off my bucket list now."

My attempt to lighten the mood didn't work. And as the hopelessness of her situation started sinking in, she went into a full-blown panic. It started with, "I don't know what I'm gonna do" and ended up at "I don't wanna live anymore". It wasn't just the things she was saying; it was the way she was saying them. The longer she talked, the less sense she was making, and it almost felt like she was losing touch with reality. It was a scary thing to watch. Then, all of a sudden, she got out of the car and said, "Go home, just leave me here. I wanna be alone!" Which freaked me out even more.

I got out too, rushed over, put my hands on her shoulders and said, "Alone is the last thing you wanna be, alright. You just gotta calm down and we'll figure this thing out."

"There's nothing to figure out. It's over!"

"No, it's not. It's never over."

"You don't understand. I'm... I'm..."

She started having trouble breathing, so I put my arms around her and started rubbing her back, which was something my Mom would do to me when I was a kid and got really worked up. I said, "It's gonna be okay, trust me."

She said, "Let me go," and tried to pull away. But I held on as tight as I could.

I spouted out whatever words came into my head, hoping something would get through to her and at some point, I said, "Look, I know it's scary, but if there was a way into this mess, that means there's a way out. And I'm gonna do whatever I can to help you find it." It was a promise made out of desperation, but it worked. I felt her body begin to settle. I guess what she needed more than anything, was to feel like she wasn't alone.

When she was as back to normal as she could get, she looked up at me and said, "Thank you."

I gave her a nod.

She said, "We should start heading back."

I agreed, and we got back in the car and headed to her school.

Once we got there, I pulled up next to her car and she started to gather her things. By that time, I was pretty confident she wasn't gonna do anything to herself, but before she left, I said, "Gimme your phone."

She said, "Why?"

"Just give it to me."

She handed it over.

I said, "Okay look, I'm gonna call you tomorrow to see how you're doing, and if you don't pick it up or call me back right away, I need somebody I can call. Someone I can tell to go check on you."

She was surprised and didn't like the idea. "No no, you don't have to do that. I just freaked out for a little bit there, that's all. I'm sorry, I'm okay now."

"Yeah, I understand, but I still need somebody I can call. So tell me who."

More than anything, I didn't wanna be in a situation where I called her the next day, and because she was feeling down and depressed and didn't wanna talk to anybody, she decided not to answer. And then I'd have to spend all day worried about whether or not she was still alive. So, this was my way to black-mail her into picking up my call.

But she still kept refusing to give me a name, so finally I said, "All right, you know what? I'm just gonna look at the last person to call you and take that person's number down."

She said, "Okay, fine."

I went to her recent calls and looked at the first name on the list: Harman Gill.

I read it again. And again. And again. Finally, I said, "How do you know this person?"

She said, "That's my brother."

I said, "Oh."

"Why? Do you know him?"

"No, no... I just uhhh... wanted to know who he was to you... in case I have to call."

I took down the number and gave her back her phone. I wasn't sure if I looked any different, but I knew I didn't feel the same. I just hoped she wouldn't notice. After thanking me again, she gave me another hug and I waited for her to get into her car, before I drove away.

But I only made it a few miles before I had to pull over to the side of the road and catch my breath. Because Jasleen's brother, Harman Gill... was Mahi's husband.

Chapter 6 – Raveena

My cousin Raveena had the misfortune of being born the third daughter in her family. Most Punjabi parents want their first-born to be a son, but if they end up having a girl, the happiness of becoming parents usually overshadows everything else. If their second child is also a girl, there's some disappointment, but they're consoled by the fact that they can try again. But if their *third* child is a girl… it's considered a tragedy. When you show up at the hospital to see the baby, you see people crying, and they aren't tears of joy. It feels less like someone was born, and more like someone died. Over time, the parents usually get over it and love that child the same as the others, but if your first impression of the world is that it doesn't want you, I imagine that's something you never forget.

Even though she was only *one* of the many female cousins I had, Raveena always stood out from the rest. The others were all obedient, 'good girls', but Raveena liked testing the boundaries of 'acceptable' Punjabi girl behavior. She'd talk back to her parents, she'd go out with her friends, she'd wear clothes that were somewhat provocative — and every time she broke the rules, she was punished a little more harshly. But she never seemed to learn her lesson.

Raveena had a special relationship with my Mom, who was the third daughter of *her* family. They both had kind of a rebellious nature, and my Mom understood the pain of being unwanted. My Mom also had miscarried a girl a few years before I was born, so she always looked at Raveena as the daughter she never had. The bond that formed between them resulted in a bond being formed between *me* and Raveena too. She spent so much time at our house that I became like a little brother to her. Maybe even more of a little brother than her actual little brother (fourth time was a charm). Since the two of us were so close, whenever she got in trouble with her parents, I'd always see everything from her side. And that carried over to the way I looked at *any* bad situation, any *other* girl was in.

Raveena was famous, or infamous, for being the first person in our entire family to choose the person she married. My parents and all my uncles and aunts had gotten arranged marriages, which was the thing to do in Punjab. When they came to America, they expected their kids to get married the same way, but America isn't Punjab, and sooner or later someone was gonna break from tradition. Raveena was that someone.

When she was in college, she met a guy from Florida in an online chat room, back when those were a thing. They hit it off right away and after a while, chatting turned into talking on the phone. A few months later, he made a surprise visit on her birthday. She couldn't believe it. He was in town for a whole week, and every day, Raveena would cut classes or sneak out of the house to go see him. By the time he went back home, Raveena had fallen for him.

But sometime during that week, a family friend saw the two of them together. And if there's one thing family friends love to do, it's deliver bad news. He told Raveena's Dad, and all hell broke loose.

Her Dad was the strict, ultra-conservative head of the family. He had this intimidating presence that terrified all of us kids when we were growing up. Whenever I was at their house, we'd be hanging out in the living room, playing video games, and as soon as we heard his car pull up outside, we'd turn off the T.V. and run upstairs.

When he found out about Raveena and her boyfriend, he reacted in character. He beat her, put her on lock down, and started making plans to take her back to Punjab to marry her off. Luckily, her boyfriend was three thousand miles away, otherwise my Uncle would've dealt with him the way they dealt with these kinds of things in the old country — by sending over a few of our most bloodthirsty family members to teach him a lesson.

Everything always goes back to one thing: "What are people gonna say?" That phrase plays a part in every aspect of a Punjabi person's life. To someone else, the 'people' in that expression might seem like some abstract thing, but it's anything but abstract. Those 'people' are people you actually know. And all Punjabis know A LOT of people.

For example, my Mom has five siblings and each of them is married. Those five couples have a combined total of 21 kids, and I grew up really close to that group of 31 cousins, uncles and aunts. Every month, we'd find some reason to get together — holidays, birthday parties, religious ceremonies, whatever. And that group of 31 was only the beginning, because my Mom also had 4 cousins who lived in the area. *That* group of couples and kids added up to 19, and I grew up almost as close to them as I did the first group. But we're still only getting started. Each of my Mom's sibling's spouses have siblings of their own. Take my Mom's sister's husband: he has six siblings, and their crew is made up of 27 people. And believe it or not, I had some kind of personal relationship with each of *them* as well. If you add up all the sibling's spouse's families, it brings the number of people in my circle to a few hundred. And I haven't even mentioned my Dad's side. Include them, and that number gets doubled. Throw in grandparents, family friends, in-laws, relatives of relatives and general acquaintances, and you're looking at close to a thousand. A thousand people who know my name.

Being connected to that many people is a special and amazing thing. It's something I took for granted until I got older and found out how rare it was. All my non-Punjabi friends would be shocked by the size our celebrations and events, and it made me realize just how small their worlds were compared to mine. Over time, I learned to appreciate what I had and treat it like a gift.

But that gift can also be a curse. Because the more people you know, the more opinions you have to consider before making any decision… and the more judgements you have to face when you make a mistake.

Every Punjabi family has someone who breaks the marriage barrier, but when it's a girl, it's a much more volatile situation. Especially with a dad like Raveena's, who was stuck on the forced marriage idea. The way he saw it, Raveena was corrupted and needed to be contained before she did any more damage to his family's reputation. He was gonna find a guy in Punjab who checked all the right boxes and marry her off as quickly as he could. Problem solved.

But luckily for Raveena, she had my parents in her corner. They were a little more liberal and open-minded and spent months trying to convince Raveena's Dad to let her marry her boyfriend. When nothing else worked, my Mom resorted to threats. She told him that not only would she not attend the forced wedding, she would cut ties with him if he went ahead with it. And when she convinced other family members to sign on to the pact, my Uncle finally gave in.

At the time, Raveena was 20 years old. And it doesn't matter who you are, or where you're from, most 20-year-olds aren't ready to get married. And in most cases, the person you're with when you're 20 isn't the person you should spend the rest of your life with. Deep inside, I think Raveena knew these things, or at least felt them, but she had just fought the biggest battle of her life and won. She didn't have it in her to fight another one. Asking for a year or two to get know her boyfriend better would have created a brand new conflict for her to deal with. She was just grateful she was being allowed to marry the person she wanted to marry, and to her, asking for anything else was asking for too much. So, she went ahead with the marriage. And even though she *chose* her husband, it turned out she made the wrong choice.

Raveena's husband's family was the traditional type and expected her to be the typical Punjabi, submissive daughter-in-law: cooking and cleaning, rarely leaving the house, always being eager to please. She tried at first, but that just wasn't her. There was constant conflict in the house and her husband, even though he was a nice guy, wasn't strong enough to stand up to his parents. Raveena was left to fend for herself, and eventually, they broke her down. But because she had fought so hard to get into this marriage in the first place, she stayed in it a lot longer than she should have, which took a toll. By the time she got divorced and came back home, she wasn't the same person. Her in-laws had taken away most of what made Raveena, *Raveena*.

When all the drama about her getting married was going on, I was just a kid. The whole thing bothered me but I was too young to be anything more than a witness. But by the time it all ended, I was a teenager. And I had picked up some of Raveena's bad habits.

Me and my family went over to see Raveena a few days after she moved back home. I could tell she wasn't the same. The light in her eyes had gone out. My parents tried their best to console her, but it was too little too late. *I* just sat there quietly, angry at everyone who was responsible for her condition. What made everything worse was that we were all gonna have to listen to my Mamma [uncle] say *I told you so*. And it didn't take him long to get started.

He was sitting next to Raveena, on the couch across from me and my parents, and as soon as there was a lull in the conversation, in Punjabi, he said, "See, this is why I was against this from the beginning. I just had a bad feeling about their family. But you all wouldn't listen, so I just decided to shut my mouth and go along with what you wanted… hoping I was wrong. But unfortunately, I wasn't." He paused and looked at Raveena, who was sitting there with her head down and nothing left to say. "But it's okay, what's done is done. We'll find someone else for her and get her married… the right way. I mean, of course it would have been a lot easier to find someone if we would've just done like this in the first place. But never mind all that. I guess we'll just have to take what we can get now."

It was bad enough listening to him act like he'd been vindicated, but hearing him talk about Raveena as if she was damaged goods was too hard to swallow. I looked around, hoping someone would speak up but they had all conceded defeat. So I felt like it was up to me. I looked at Raveena and said, "Is that okay with you Raveena?"

Everyone, including Raveena, was taken aback. Why was this kid getting involved in an adult conversation? My Uncle looked at me like I was a pest and said, "Why wouldn't she be okay with it?"

I ignored him and continued talking to Raveena. "Look, you're still young, you can marry any guy you want. Just go out there, take your time and find the right one."

The more I talked, the redder my Uncle's face became. And it takes a lot for a brown person's face to turn red. He said, "Who the hell's asking *you?*"

I kept going. "It's just a divorce, it's not a big deal. You don't gotta feel bad about it."

Finally, he got fed up. "I'm talking to you!"

I said, "Well I'm not talking to *you* Mamma ji, I'm talking to *her.*"

Everyone in the room gasped. My Mom snapped at me, trying to put an end to whatever it was I was doing. My Uncle was furious. He said, "What did you say?"

I went back to Raveena. "You didn't do nothing wrong, Raveena. So you don't have to do anything you don't wanna do. Don't listen to what anyone says."

My Uncle looked at my Dad and said, "Jeet, you better control your boy, otherwise—"

I cut him off. "Otherwise what? What are you gonna do?"

It didn't take long for him to show me. He stood up, marched over and smacked me across the face.

One of the commandments of Punjabi culture is that you respect your elders no matter what. You can argue with them to a certain extent, but there's a line you never cross. You learn early on where exactly that line is, and you're taught to be terrified of what's on the other side. Now, all of a sudden, I found myself on the other side. At first, it was scary, but as I sat there, looking around at everyone's stunned faces, I started to get this strange feeling that this was the side I belonged on. And I figured that since there was no going back, I might as well go further.

I stood up, looked deep into my Uncle's bulging, red eyes… and smacked him back.

Chaos followed. Everyone jumped in between us, yelling and screaming, but there wasn't really a fight to break up. Both me and my Uncle were completely still, in shock over what had just happened. Because it wasn't supposed to happen. It wasn't supposed to be possible.

I wasn't proud of what I did. Hitting your uncle is nothing to be proud of. But at the same time, I didn't regret it either, because it taught me an important lesson — not every elder deserves respect. 'Respect your elders' is just something they tell you so they don't have to go through the trouble of actually *earning* your respect. It's a rule they teach you as early as possible so you never think to question it. You're led to believe that the consequence of breaking that rule is some kind of death. But I broke it and I was still alive. And I was more alive than I had ever been.

After the incident, my Mom didn't talk to me for a few months, which was hard, but eventually she came around.

Moms always do. Raveena, on the other hand, never did. Her family cut ties with us, so she had to pick a side, and she picked them. I couldn't blame her though. Her Dad was still her dad after all, and what I did to him was unforgiveable. He ended up finding a guy for her, just like he said he would, and she's been married to him ever since. She even has a couple of kids now, and who knows, she might even be happy. But she deserved so much more.

Raveena's first boyfriend wasn't fit to be her husband. That's supposed to be a normal part of life. But in her case, it was a crime she was punished for. I didn't know much back then, but I knew how wrong and unfair that was. Of all the freedoms a person should have, the freedom to make mistakes is one of the most important. And that's a freedom girls don't usually get. The world is so eager to label them as 'bad' that all it takes is one slip-up to earn that title. Even the ones who rebel and embrace the 'bad', usually just get stuck in a never-ending rebellion. But rebellion is supposed to be a steppingstone towards independence and equality, not a way of life. When it turns into that, you're still being controlled by the ones you're rebelling against. So the only choice you have is to be perfect. And if you're anything short of that, you end up like Raveena.

Chapter 7 – What If You Could?

I always felt like everyone else was moving, and I was standing still. Like *they* all knew where they were going and how to get there, and I was the only one with nowhere to go. Every time I tried to find my way, I ended up back where I started, and after a while, I had to wonder if there was even a 'way' to be found. If maybe some souls are just meant to be lost. And the closest they can ever get to finding their place in the world, is by keeping someone else from losing theirs.

The next morning, I called Jasleen and she answered immediately. My blackmail trick worked. She sounded down and depressed, but she also sounded alive, and that's all that mattered to me. I asked her if she wanted to hang out after school, and she said, "Okay."

That evening, we met up at this hipster coffee shop near her school. She wanted to meet somewhere private, but I insisted on a public place because I figured she was less likely to become hysterical with people around. I got there a little early and ordered my coffee. Just as I sat down by the window, she pulled into the parking lot, and I was glad she was on time. A little longer alone with my thoughts, and I might've talked myself out of what I was about to do.

As she stepped out of her car, I noticed she looked somewhat better. Her hair was done up, she was wearing a striped pink cardigan and fancy jeans, and she seemed more human than zombie, unlike the previous couple days. But as soon as she saw my face, a look of dread came over her. Being at school all day was an escape, but I was a reminder of her reality.

The paranoia kicked in soon after that too. Before she even sat down, she noticed a girl sitting a few tables away who kinda looked Punjabi and said, "Dude, that girl keeps staring at me."

I turned and looked. "Maybe she's into you."

"It's not funny. I'm serious."

"Just sit down. She's not even looking this way."

"Let's go somewhere else."

"For real?"

"Yes."

I tried telling her she was imagining things, but Jasleen was adamant about leaving, and we ended up walking to a small park across the street.

Once we got there, we sat down on a bench and I asked, "So have you thought about what you're gonna do?"

She said, "I've been trying *not* to think about what I'm gonna do. There's nothing I really *can* do. I just wanna live normally for as long as possible, and then I'm gonna have to tell my parents. And after that… my life's over."

"How do you know that?"

"Because I do."

"Are you a psychic or something?"

"I know my Dad. He's gonna kill me when he finds out."

"Is he *literally* gonna kill you?"

She looked at me and rolled her eyes.

I took a couple sips of my coffee. "How is your Dad? I mean, like, how strict is he?"

"Very. Like the whole time I was with my ex, I was scared to death of him finding out. Even if I was ready to get married, it would have been hard for me to tell him. And that's just a boyfriend. Can you imagine if I told him I was pregnant?"

I nodded.

"And the thing is, even if I wanted to tell'em *that*, I don't know how, because I can't tell'em who the fuckin' father is."

We were the only ones in the park, except for a few pigeons walking through the grass. I watched them until they flew away. Then, I turned to Jasleen, gave her a long stare and said, "What if you could?"

"I already told you I don't want to have anything to do with him ever again."

"I'm not talking about *him*."

"What do you mean?"

I took a breath, and said, "What if *I* was the father?"

She was taken aback. "But you're not."

"What if I was?

"But you're NOT."

"Look, *you* know that... and *I* know that... but nobody else does. So what if I just pretended to be?"

When I heard the words out loud, I was almost as surprised as Jasleen was.

She looked at me like I was crazy and said, "Listen, I really appreciate what you did for me yesterday, but I would never ever ask you to do that."

I said, "What if I *wanted* to do it?"

"Why would you want to? You met me like two weeks ago.

55

And if I remember correctly, you gave me this whole speech about how you didn't even wanna be my boyfriend. And now you wanna raise a *kid* with me?"

I put down my coffee cup and was quiet for a moment. Then I turned back to her and said, "Why'd you stop talking to me?"

She thought about it and said, "Uhh, because I found out I was pregnant."

"So?"

"What do you mean, so?"

"Why was that a reason?"

"Because it changes everything."

"Not for me."

She gave me a confused look. "Seriously? How can it not?"

I shrugged. "It just doesn't. The way I see it... I met you, I liked you and I was starting to get to know you. And before I found out you were pregnant, I wanted to *keep* getting to know you. And now that I know you *are*... I still want to."

"Okay, but you still didn't answer my question. Why would you wanna pretend to be the father of my baby?"

"Because you need someone to... and I got nothing better to do."

"Really? That's your reason?"

"Yeah, it is. Of all the things I could do with my life... I can't think of anything better."

She shook her head in frustration. "But what would that mean? How long would you pretend? Forever? Are you gonna marry me?"

"To tell you the truth, I really don't know what it means. What I *do* know is... if you're keeping this baby, then sooner or later you're gonna have to tell your parents. And if you're gonna tell your parents, you have to tell'em who the father is. Right now, you can't do that, but I can make it so you can. And after that, we'll just take whatever comes our way and deal with it. The only thing I can tell you for sure is, I'll be *with* you through all of this… as long as you *want* me with you. I won't abandon you. That much I can promise."

She took a moment to let what I was saying sink in. "Look, I don't think you understand what you're trying to sign up for okay. You're acting like this is just gonna be some small inconvenience for you, but this is something that would change your whole life. You know that, right?"

"Yeah, I do. But maybe my life needs a change."

"Okay, then go back to school, or find a new job. That's what normal people do."

I laughed. "I guess I'm not normal then."

"Yeah, clearly." She gave me a long stare, then said, "Why are you pretending this isn't a big deal?"

"I'm not. I know it's a big deal. But I also know it's not the end of the world."

"See that's the part you're not getting though. For me, it *is* the end of the world."

"Well, I disagree."

She sighed.

"But let's just say you're right and I'm wrong… and the world really *is* gonna end. Do you really wanna be alone when it happens? Wouldn't you rather have someone *with* you?"

As much as she didn't wanna drag me into her mess, she also didn't wanna spend the rest of her life with her ex-boyfriend. And she knew that was gonna be her only other choice.

So, once she realized she couldn't talk me out of my crazy idea, she stopped trying to talk *herself* out of it too. And she accepted my proposal.

She might have thought I was out of my mind. That I was throwing my life away for no rhyme or reason and had no idea what I was getting myself into. But *she* was the one who didn't know what was coming. I had already seen this story. I knew exactly how it was gonna play out. How they were gonna break her down until she was completely broken. But I also knew it wasn't their anger, or pressure, or judgement that would do her in… it was her own shame. And after watching *one* girl drown in her own shame, I wasn't gonna let it happen to another.

Chapter 8 – The Gill Family

There's a reason Punjabi girls are paranoid in public — their enemies are always watching. And every Punjabi girl has a lot of enemies. Many of whom they barely even know. Gossiping aunties, overbearing uncles, hater distant cousins, jealous friends of friends. It doesn't matter where you go, or how careful you think you're being, there's always the possibility that one of *them* could spot you. And if they happen to catch you slippin'... they'll do whatever they can to see you fall.

Jasleen was with her ex-boyfriend for four years and somehow managed to keep it a secret the whole time. Me and her didn't make it four *weeks*. Because that random Punjabi-looking girl, in that random coffee shop we met up at, turned out to be the daughter of a friend of Jasleen's Aunt. And naturally, she had to tell her mom what she saw.

When I told Jasleen she had nothing to worry about, I didn't realize who her family was. I had heard Mahi married into a rich family, but these guys weren't any regular kind of rich. They lived in a mansion in the San Jose hills and were one of the most well-known families in the community. Jasleen's Dad owned 17 gas stations across three states and every Punjabi in San Jose, from the Gurdwara to the grocery store, knew who he was. Me,

I never paid attention to those kinds of things so I had no idea — but I was one of the few who didn't.

I guess I couldn't blame Jasleen for not telling me. It probably would've been a little weird for her to say "Hey, you know I'm a little more recognizable than your average girl?" But apparently she was exactly that, and it was a part of her life she always hated.

It's hard enough being the regular daughter of a regular strict Punjabi father, but when your father's a big deal, the pressure is on another level. At that point, you can't afford to make even the smallest mistake because people are *looking* to bring you down. Jasleen's Dad was always very conscious of that and he made sure everyone else in the household was too. And anyone he thought was *extra* prone to making mistakes got *extra* reminders.

As for the Aunt who found out about us — she wasn't just some random aunt. She was the wife of Jasleen's Dad's older brother, and the two of them had been thorns in Jasleen's side since the day they came to America. Jasleen was in elementary school when her Uncle's family immigrated, and by that time, her Dad was already a huge success. But the Uncle felt like he was entitled to some of that wealth, so the Dad made him a partner in the business and ever since then, the two families had basically been one.

There was always a love/hate relationship between them though. Since he was the oldest, the Uncle considered himself the head of the family and had a habit of meddling in everyone's lives, which caused a lot of problems, especially with Jasleen. He had two daughters of his own but they grew up in a village in Punjab, so an outspoken, outgoing, California girl like Jasleen was a shock to his system. To him, she was someone who needed to be 'fixed', because in his eyes, a girl with anything other than a submissive attitude was a girl who was out of control. He was always pushing her Dad to tighten the reins on her, and Jasleen ended up having even *more* restrictions placed on her than she had to begin with.

And then there was the Aunt, whose sole mission in life was to prove she was better than Jasleen's Mom. Sisters-in-law in the same family are usually in competition with each other, but Jasleen's Mom was pretty mild-mannered and wanted no part in any of that. The Aunt saw it differently. She would try to outdo her any chance she got, and her favorite way to show her superiority was through her kids. If Jasleen's parents threw her or Harman a birthday party, the Aunt would throw a bigger party for her *own* kids when *their* birthdays came around. If Harman or Jasleen did well in school, the Aunt would get her kids private tutors so *their* grades would be even better. She made sure her kids wore fancier clothes, drove flashier cars, and had finer things. She'd use every opportunity to praise *her* kids, and put down Jasleen and Harman, so when she heard about *us*, it must have been like finding a winning lottery ticket. And you better believe she was gonna cash that thing in the most dramatic way possible.

One day, the Aunt came over to Jasleen's house carrying a big stack of colorful outfits. There was a huge party happening at the end of the month for Jasleen's parents' 30th anniversary and the Aunt wanted to get an opinion on what to wear. But as Jasleen went through the collection, the Aunt started saying strange things like, "You're the only daughter I have left now" (by then, her two daughters were both married and had moved

61

away) and "You can always come to me if you ever need to talk about anything." Then she randomly explained, "You know, I actually have a much more modern way of thinking than your parents do. They're kind of old-fashioned." None of it made any sense to Jasleen, but all of it made her nervous. Finally, the Aunt said, "So have you thought about marriage at all?"

Jasleen was taken aback. "Marriage? What? No, I'm way too young."

"Well, I mean, if your parents find out what you're up to... that might not matter."

"Huh? What do you mean 'up to'? I'm not 'up to' anything."

The Aunt put her hand on Jasleen's shoulder and in Punjabi said, "Listen dear, you don't have to pretend with me... I already know everything."

All Jasleen wanted was a few weeks to act like her life was still normal, but that turned out to be too much to ask. At first, she tried to deny everything, but her Aunt didn't buy it, so Jasleen ended up admitting that me and her were 'seeing each other' and begged her Aunt not to tell her parents. Her Aunt said, "She would never even dream of doing such a thing" and only wanted what was "best for Jasleen", but Jasleen knew better than to believe all that. The niceness was probably part of some grander scheme and it was obvious that if she didn't talk to her parents soon, they would end up 'finding out'.

Once the Aunt left, Jasleen called me to tell me what happened. I was at the restaurant and stepped out to take the call, and as soon as the conversation started, I sensed a tone in her voice I had never heard before. After explaining the situation, she said, "See this is why I didn't wanna meet up in public."

It kinda caught me off guard. Was she really trying to say it was *my* fault her Aunt found out? I said, "Well there was no way anyone could've known this random chick was gonna know who you are?"

"Yeah, but if you would've just listened to me in the first place, it wouldn't have mattered."

Okay, now I was *sure* she was blaming me. I said, "Yo, the odds of all this happening were like one in a million, so maybe it was just a thing that was meant to be."

"That's easy for you to say… you're not the one dealing with it!"

"Yeah, but I *am* trying to *help* you deal with it."

"Well if you really wanna help me, try LISTENING to what I tell you next time."

"Bitch, what?!" is what I wanted to say. But instead I went with, "Are you for real? Are you actually trying to blame me for this?"

"I'm not blaming you. I'm just stating the facts."

"The facts? Okay, how about this fact — what was I *doing* at that coffee shop to begin with? I was helping you figure out what to do about *your* situation. What about the day before? What was I doing? I was taking you to an abortion clinic. Did you forget about those facts?"

"Look, I didn't *force* you to do any of that okay, I just *asked*. If you didn't want to, you could've just said no!"

"I'm not saying I didn't want to. I just don't understand how you can ignore all that shit."

"I'm not ignoring it, I'm just…" She started to cry. "I'm going through so much right now, and I don't know what I'm gonna do. So I don't need you yelling at me."

"I'm not ye—"

"Like no matter how hard I try to be positive about it, I can't see how anything in my life's ever gonna be okay again."

I softened my tone a bit. "Listen, I get that it's hard, I really do, but all I'm saying is… I'm *with* you in all this, I'm not *against* you. So don't be against *me*."

She didn't respond. There was a long silence and then she said, "I gotta go help my Mom with dinner… I'll talk to you later."

After that phone call, I was a lot of things — angry, frustrated, exhausted — but more than anything, I was disillusioned. I didn't recognize the girl I had just talked to. It was a side of her I had never seen before and I started to think, "Was this who she really was?" "Is *this* the girl I got myself involved with?" They were scary thoughts and for the next few hours, I couldn't get'em out of my mind. Up until then, all my feelings towards Jasleen were positive, but now I was filled with this weird hostility towards her.

Later that night, just as I was about to go to sleep, my phone started to ring. Normally, when I looked down at my phone and it said 'Jasleen calling', I'd be excited to pick up, but this time I just wanted to let it keep ringing. I did for a while… but then I decided I should answer. I said, "Hello," as unenthusiastically as possible.

She said, "Hey."

"What's up?"

"Nothing." She was quiet for a moment, then said, "Hey sorry about earlier… I didn't really mean all that stuff I said."

Not what I was expecting to hear. I said, "Uhh… yeah, no… it's cool."

She said, "No, it's not. Here you are, trying to help me out, and I'm being a fuckin' bitch to you. That's not right, and you don't deserve that. Everything just kinda got to me and I lost it, but still, I mean… that's no excuse."

"Uhh, yeah. It's all good, you know."

"Are you mad?"

"Nah… I mean, I understand."

"Okay. But just so you know, I really do appreciate whatever you're doing. I mean, I still think you're a crazy person for doing it… but I'm glad you are."

"Yeah… okay."

"Alright, umm… goodnight."

Up until that point, I had never been in a long-term relationship, so I hadn't spent enough time with a girl to actually learn how one operates. If a girl was being irrational, it just meant that she was an irrational person, and not someone I wanted to be around. I didn't know anything about hormones and periods and how powerful those types of things are. How they can temporarily transform a girl into someone else. And in this case, I was dealing with a girl who was pregnant, so all of that was on another level. But me, I was completely oblivious to it and I went to sleep that night confused about what the hell had just happened. I was just glad Jasleen was back to being Jasleen.

* * *

I don't know what it is about dads that makes them so hard to talk to. Even with *my* Dad, who's a relatively reasonable guy, there were always certain things I couldn't bring myself to tell'em. If I wanted something from my parents, or I needed to deliver some bad news, I wouldn't just go talk to the both of them — I'd tell my Mom and let *her* tell my Dad. It just seemed like the easier way to go. So when it came to Jasleen telling her parents about her 'boyfriend', we both agreed that was the best approach to take.

One morning, during breakfast, when nobody but the two of them were home, Jasleen told her Mom she wanted to talk to her about something. Right away, her Mom got nervous. She was the worrying type so she automatically assumed it was something bad, especially since Jasleen had never started a conversation with those words before. After beating around the bush for a bit, Jasleen finally worked up the courage to say, "There's a guy... I've been seeing." Her Mom was taken aback and started bombarding her with questions. "Who is he?" "Where did you meet him?" "What does he do?" Jasleen told her all about me and tried her hardest to paint me in the best light.

All moms have two sides to them — the side that wants you to follow the rules, and the side that wants you to get married as soon as possible. And when the two sides are pitted against each other, the 'get married' side will win every time. As much as Jasleen's Mom wanted to play the role of the disappointed parent, her excitement about a possible wedding wouldn't let that happen. And once she found out I wasn't a criminal and didn't belong to a different race or religion, she was sold. By the end of the conversation she had given Jasleen her stamp of approval and told her she was happy for her. The easy part was over.

All day at school, the only thing Jasleen could think about

was her Mom telling her Dad. And every time she pictured it, a chill ran down her spine. According to Jasleen, her Dad was a good guy — he just didn't show a lot of affection or emotion, so it was always hard to figure out what he was thinking. He had a quiet intensity that made him uncomfortable to be around. But even though he didn't express it, her and Harman always *felt* his love. When they were kids, he would take them on trips and buy them the latest games or toys. It wasn't so much about the places they went or the stuff he bought; it was the fact that he made the effort to do those things that they appreciated.

As they got older though, the relationship began to change — especially with Jasleen. Harman was the perfect child: a straight-A student, who was respectful and responsible and someone you never had to worry about. Jasleen was a different story. She was bold. And a bold brown girl is always a problem.

In her freshman year of high school, Jasleen joined a co-ed bhangra team without telling her parents. She had always been really into dancing and had a reputation for being good at it. At family parties, she'd be the star of the dancefloor, and friends and relatives were always encouraging her to do something with her talent. Unfortunately though, her Dad wasn't a fan of the idea. In his mind, dance was not something that girls from 'good families' got involved in, so he wouldn't allow it.

But when the opportunity to join a bhangra team came along, Jasleen couldn't bring herself to turn it down. She decided to join, thinking she'd be able to keep it a secret. She thought wrong. A couple weeks into it, her Dad found out and completely flipped out. Instead of confronting her at home though, he showed up to one of her practices unannounced, yelled at her in front of her teammates and forced her to quit on the spot.

It was a traumatic experience for Jasleen, and she said her relationship with her Dad was never the same again. She was filled with a weird mix of fear and resentment towards him. On one hand, she would go out of her way to do things she knew he wouldn't approve of, but on the other, she'd be scared to death of him finding out about those things.

The older she got, the more her Dad treated her, and talked to her, and looked at her like there was something wrong with her. And Jasleen was always stuck between trying to prove there *wasn't*... and being afraid there *was*.

That night, when Jasleen got home from school, her Dad was sitting in the living room, watching TV, waiting for her. He wasn't happy. After having her take a seat, in Punjabi he asked, "So what's all this your Mom's talking about?" When Jasleen didn't respond, he continued, "Is this what we sent you to school for? Are these the kinds of things you do there?" Her Mom came into the room and told him to take it easy on her, but he quickly shut her down. "*You* shouldn't say anything, you're the reason this all happened."

That's when Jasleen finally opened her mouth. For whatever reason, it was always easier for her to speak up for other people than speak up for *herself*. She said, "Don't blame *her* Dad. It's not her fault."

He said, "Then whose fault is it? Mine?"

"No... it's nobody's fault... it just happened."

Eventually, her Dad started asking her his *own* set of questions about me. And his were a little more harsh. "How much does he make?" "Can he afford to support you?" "Does he know who we are?" "How do you know he's not after our money?"

Jasleen did her best to answer and considering the fact that 'having a boyfriend' was only half the story, and she was so afraid of her Dad, it wouldn't have been surprising if she crumbled under the pressure. But she managed to hold herself together long enough to convince him to give me a chance. At the end of the conversation, he said, "Have him come over… we'll talk."

Afterwards, she called me to tell me how everything went and said her parents wanted to meet me that weekend. She asked if that would work, but when I told her it would, she went silent.

I said, "Hello?

She said, "Yeah, umm… are you sure? I mean, we can do some other time if you're busy?"

"No, this weekend's good. I'm free."

"Oh… okay."

Ever since she saw those two lines on the pregnancy test, she had been having nightmares about the moment she'd tell her parents. The only thing that made her life any easier was knowing that moment was somewhere far away. But now it was here.

I said, "Are you alright?"

She didn't respond for a while, then said, "Is this really about to happen?"

"I think so."

"Does it have to?"

"Sooner or later… yeah."

"Why couldn't it be later? Why couldn't that bitch have just kept her mouth shut?"

"I don't know. But if she did, you probably would've just spent more time regretting everything that happened, and dreading everything that's about to. So maybe it was a good thing."

She sighed. "I don't even know how I'm gonna make those words come out of my mouth."

"Well, if there's one thing I know you're good at, it's making words come out of your mouth. So I think you'll find a way."

I managed to get the slightest laugh out of her, then she went back to being quiet. A few moments later, she said, "Tell me honestly, are you saying all this just to make me feel better, or do you really believe everything's gonna be okay?"

I thought about it for a moment. "Look, I can't say I believe *everything's* gonna be okay. Everything is a lot. I just believe *you're* gonna be okay."

"Why?"

"Because you're hard not to believe in."

Despite everything Jasleen had to deal with growing up — her strict Dad, her family's status, her crazy Uncle and Aunt — she still had the courage to sneak around with a boyfriend for all those years. As great as her fear was, it couldn't stop her from being true to who she was. And a girl who was true to herself is worth putting your faith in.

Chapter 9 – Enemy Territory

Driving to a rich person's house is a unique experience. It starts out just like any other drive — there's lights, there's traffic, there's pedestrians. But the further you go, the quieter everything becomes, until eventually, it's just you and a road on a hill. And by the time you get there, it's like you left one world and entered another. I wonder what it is about becoming successful that makes you wanna get away from everyone else.

The house was even bigger than I thought it would be. Or maybe my imagination was too small. As I drove through the gate and down the exaggeratedly long driveway, I felt like a commoner approaching a castle. Maybe it was just me, but it almost seemed like the place was *built* to make you feel that way. Like your existence didn't even matter. I don't know if intimidation was what they were going for, but that's what they got, and to get over it I had to take a moment to remind myself why I was there. I had to remind myself that a few weeks earlier I met a girl I really liked, and now she wasn't here anymore. And it was her fear of the people in that house that made her disappear. All I wanted to do was bring her back.

Jasleen had made it clear she wanted only her parents to meet me and nobody else, but when I got to the porch, there were a few more pairs of shoes on the ground than I was expecting. Before I could even ring the bell, Jasleen opened the door. It was the first time I had ever seen her in a Punjabi suit and I remember being struck by how good she looked in one. But before I could give her a compliment, she gave me some bad news — her Uncle's family was there too. Apparently word got out that Jasleen was bringing a guy over and they invited themselves to the party. It wasn't clear who told'em, but Jasleen was pretty sure it was her Grandma, who was always going back and forth between the two houses, leaking confidential information. Punjabi grandmas only come in two varieties — good ones and evil ones. And Jasleen's was one of the latter.

So now Jasleen, who was already a nervous wreck, was on the verge of a breakdown. She said, "Maybe we shouldn't tell'em today."

I said, "Then when would we?"

"I don't know. Some other time."

"I mean, it's up to you, but it's just a few more people, and they're gonna find out anyway."

"Yeah but—"

She was cut off by an obnoxiously loud voice coming from inside. The voice, which was her Aunt's, said in Punjabi, "Are you gonna let him in or make him stand outside the whole time?"

I looked at Jasleen and said, "We'll just see what happens."

She still wasn't sure, but there was no more time to discuss it and she led me inside.

Even though the house was more than triple the size of mine and a thousand times as fancy, it still had a lot of the same touches every Punjabi home had — the gold elephant statues, the tall vases with giant peacock feathers sticking out of them, the pictures of Sikh gurus on the walls. It was a strange mix of foreign and familiar.

We got to the living room where three ladies were waiting for me — her Mom, her Aunt, and her Grandma. They all greeted me with big smiles and sat me down. The Aunt and Grandma came off just as sketchy as they were described. They called me by my name, Inderjit, which I thought was weird. It was like they were trying too hard to create familiarity between us. But there was a sincerity to Jasleen's Mom that reminded me of my *own* Mom. She had this round, kind face and seemed like the type who could forgive you for just about anything. And her kindness made me second guess what we were about to do. The thought of telling Jasleen's parents about the pregnancy didn't faze me at all when it was just a thought. But actually looking into the eyes of someone who would be devastated by the news put everything in a different perspective.

Luckily, the men walked in soon afterwards and got my mind back on track. The dead-serious looks on their faces completely changed the mood in the room. If Jasleen's Mom was trying to make me feel at home, *they* wanted me to know I was in enemy territory. I got up and shook each one of their hands, but there were no smiles or pleasantries. They were all business.

Jasleen's Dad had these eyes you couldn't penetrate and a demeanor that said 'it's no use even trying'. He was shorter than I thought he would be, but that somehow made him even *more* intimidating. According to Jasleen there was a big heart underneath the rough exterior, but I couldn't see any signs of it, and I don't think he wanted me to.

The Uncle was the complete opposite. If I didn't know they

were brothers, I wouldn't have believed it. He was half a foot taller and had all the charisma the Dad didn't. But it was like a shady politician's charisma. The kind you knew better than to trust. He looked like someone who could make bad things happen to you. The third and final member of the crew was his stocky, mean-muggin' son, Satti. Satti was like an older brother to Jasleen and Harman growing up, but not the type that helped you with your homework or taught you how to throw a football. He was more the type to boss you around and embarrass you in front of your friends. Even if Jasleen hadn't told me all of that about him, I would've guessed it just by looking at him. For some reason, bullies all have that same face. You almost can't blame'em for turning out the way they do.

We all sat down and the chatter in the room was replaced by a tense silence. The interrogation was about to begin so I turned to Jasleen to give her some last-second reassurance... but she already looked defeated.

The Dad spoke first. In Punjabi, he said, "So Jasleen tells me your family owns a restaurant?"

I said, "Yeah, we've had it since I was a kid. It's called 'Rasoi'."

"Hmm... never heard of it."

Maybe he meant it as an insult, but I was actually glad he had never heard of it. The less he knew about my family, the better.

I said, "Yeah it's just a small place."

Apparently, it wasn't too small for Satti to know about. He said, "That's over there off Alum Rock, right?"

I nodded. "That's the one."

"Yeah, I haven't been there... maybe I'll check it out one of

74

these days."

He said it as if he'd be doing me an honor by stopping by. I said, "Come through anytime man."

Then the Uncle jumped in. "So are you just working there or are you going to school too?"

"Nah, I'm done with school."

"Oh... what did you graduate in?"

"I didn't graduate."

"Why not?"

"I don't know... I just wasn't that into school."

He gave me a dickish smile and said, "You weren't into it or it was too hard for you?"

I smiled back and said, "Maybe both."

Jasleen's Mom decided to help me out. She said, "That's okay, school's not for everyone."

And then the Aunt gave an example to back her up. "Yeah, just look at your cousin Tanveer's brother-in-law. What was his name again? Ballu? He dropped out of college and started his own company, and now he's a millionaire."

Satti let out a laugh. "Yeah, exactly." He pointed at me. "I'm sure *he's* gonna do the same thing."

The Dad wasn't convinced though. He said, "So are you just planning on working at the restaurant your whole life, or do you have some other plans for the future?"

I shrugged. "I don't know... no one can predict the future."

"What does that mean?"

"It means anything can happen."

"That's it? You're just hoping something happens? Look, things don't just happen, okay, you gotta make them happen." He looked around at his house. "All of this didn't just fall out of the sky. I had to work for it, I had to plan for it. So maybe you should start thinking about what you wanna do with your life."

I nodded. "Good advice."

He didn't appreciate my attitude. None of them did. I think they were all expecting me to be desperate for their approval, but I was just treating it like a casual conversation, which is what it was to me. I didn't come there looking for anything, because they didn't have anything I needed.

There was a bit of an awkward silence until out of left field, the Grandma decided to throw out a classic 'grandma' question: "What village in Punjab is your family from?" This was the first thing every older Punjabi person wanted to know whenever they met someone new. It was also a sneaky way to find out what caste I belonged to. I told her, and that started up a brand new line of questioning about my family history and lineage.

With every answer I gave them, they liked me less. If there was an image in their mind of who they *didn't* want as a son-in-law, *I* would be it. Uneducated, middle-class, no fancy job, different caste — and the worst news was yet to come.

About 30 minutes into it, there was a break in the conversation. The ladies went into the kitchen and one by one, the men left the room too. First Satti stepped out to make a phone call, then the Uncle joined the ladies in the kitchen, and the Dad went to the bathroom. Me and Jasleen were left alone, so I turned to her and asked, "So when do you wanna tell'em?"

She said, "I don't know. I don't know *how* to. Maybe I'll just tell my parents later, when everyone's gone."

"You really wanna do it by yourself?"

"It's okay... it'll be fine."

"But how's that gonna make *me* look? Coming here and

leaving without mentioning something as big as that? They're never gonna have any respect for me if I do that."

"Maybe I should've just told Harman and had *him* talk to them."

"Yeah, maybe, I don't know... but it's too late for that now."

That's when we heard a voice say, "Too late for what?" It was Satti, walking back into the room. "What are you guys talking about?"

I said, "Uhh nothing man, we were just... talking."

"Sounds like something serious." He noticed the concern on Jasleen's face. "Everything cool Jasleen?"

I said, "Yeah, everything's good bro."

"I'm not talking to you, I'm talking to her."

As he said that, the Uncle came back in and noticed the tension. He said, "*Ki hogaya?*[What happened?]"

Satti said, "I don't know... they were talking about something and Jasleen got upset."

The ladies came back into the room with trays full of samosas, chutneys, sweets and cha and placed them on the table. Then the Dad showed up, just in time to hear the Uncle ask, "What's wrong Jasleen?"

Jasleen was overwhelmed by the sight of everyone staring down at her. She looked at her Uncle and said, "Nothing," but as she said it, her voice cracked and it was obvious to everyone she wasn't telling the truth. They all got worried and started pressing her for an answer. "Did something happen?" "Are you okay?" She couldn't bring herself to respond. Then tears started coming down her face, which freaked them out even more. Since they couldn't get an explanation out of her, they turned to me for one. "What's going on?" "What did you say to her?"

I didn't wanna be the one to tell'em. It wasn't my place. So I kept looking over at Jasleen, hoping she'd say something, but there were no signs she was going to. And the longer the two of us kept quiet, the more aggressive they got with me. "Speak up!" "Why aren't you saying anything?"

Finally, I said, "Okay, listen…"

They quieted down.

"There's something else we have to tell you." I looked at Jasleen again to give her one last chance. She didn't take it. I turned back to them and said, "The thing is… Jasleen… she's… she's pregnant."

I expected some huge outcry… but there was absolute silence. It wasn't shock or devastation, it was something I didn't even recognize. Something none of them knew what to do with. I looked at each of them, trying to find any hint of a reaction, but all I saw were blank faces… until I got to Jasleen's Dad. He was standing all the way in the back, shaking. It was like seeing a ticking timebomb the moment before it exploded.

He looked at Jasleen and said, "What did he say?"

She couldn't respond.

"Is it true?"

Jasleen gave him the slightest nod of her head… and that's all it took. Suddenly, he came rushing towards us. I thought he was gonna hit Jasleen, so I immediately got up to shield her, but it wasn't *her* he was coming after… it was *me*. He put his hand around my throat and started choking me as hard as he could. A huge commotion erupted, and I didn't know what to do. Fighting back wasn't an option, so I waited for the others to pull him off me, which they eventually did. As everyone tried to settle him down, he shouted at Jasleen in Punjabi, "Get out of here!"

Jasleen's Mom grabbed him by the arm and said, "Stop it! What are you doing?"

He said, "Tell them to leave right now! Otherwise… otherwise don't blame me for what I do!"

It was obvious to me we weren't gonna reach an understanding that day, so I turned to Jasleen, who was in a state of shock, and said, "We should go." But she couldn't take her eyes off her Dad, who was still yelling and screaming. I said, "Jasleen!" Finally, she turned to me and I made a gesture towards the front door. She got what I was saying, put her hand in mine and stood up.

Her Mom noticed us and said, "Wait, just hold on a second."

I said, "I'm really sorry Auntie ji… but this isn't gonna end well if we stay."

Then she turned to Jasleen and said, "How could you do this?"

Jasleen still couldn't bring herself to speak, but she tried as hard as she could to apologize with her eyes as I rushed her out of the house.

Every Punjabi girl knows she's destined to leave her home someday, but none ever imagine it happening like that. And it's even worse when you feel like you don't deserve any better.

I drove around aimlessly, trying to console Jasleen, who was completely devastated. It took hours, but she finally pulled herself together enough to call her friend Candice, the angry blonde from the night we met. She told her what happened and Candice decided Jasleen was gonna stay at her apartment until she could figure things out. Jasleen tried turning her down, but Candice wasn't taking no for answer, and Jasleen eventually gave in.

When we pulled up to the apartment building, Jasleen apologized to me. I said, "Don't trip, I've been through worse." Getting choked wasn't fun, but it was nothing compared to what happened to her. I knew the marks on my neck were gonna heal, but I wasn't so sure *she* would. Still though, I did my best to give her some hope. I said, "Look, I know you feel like shit right now, but the hardest part's over... things can only get better from here." I don't think she believed me, but she leaned over to give me a hug, then got out of the car and disappeared into the building.

When most people hug, they don't put their *all* into it. But Jasleen always squeezed as hard as she could. It didn't seem fair that someone who gave so much of herself could get so little in return.

Chapter 10 – A World With You In It

That night, Jasleen got two phone calls. The first was from her Mom, who wanted to know where she was, how she was doing and most importantly, how she could let all this happen. Jasleen did her best to explain and apologize, but even the most understanding person in the world can only understand so much. Her Mom was disappointed in her and let her know it, which made Jasleen feel even worse than she already did.

The second call was from her brother. By then, he had heard the news and was upset with Jasleen for keeping him in the dark. She told him she didn't wanna put him in the middle of it all, but he said she would've been much better off if she had. After the way everything went down, that was hard to argue with. He told her to hang tight and promised to drive down and have a talk with the parents. And the next day, he did just that.

In the evening, he called Jasleen again and said he wanted to come by Candice's place to talk to the both of us. And that was the day I met Mahi's husband for the first time.

Candice's apartment was a small but modern spot in the quieter part of downtown. When I got there, her and Jasleen were in the kitchen cooking dinner and Harman still hadn't arrived. The whole place smelled like pasta. Based on my first encounter with Candice, I figured she would hate me. She didn't seem to think highly of dudes in general and I was the asshole who got her friend pregnant. But it turned out Jasleen told her the truth, which made me 'one of the good ones' in her eyes. We got a chance to talk in private for a few minutes while Jasleen went into the bedroom to take a phone call, and she thanked me for what I was doing. She said, "I know it's probably been hard for you, but just so you know, it's a worthwhile cause. Jasleen's a really special girl."

It was strange talking to a third person about everything going on, because up until then, it was all just between me and Jasleen. But it was nice to get some outside reassurance that I wasn't out of my mind for doing what I was doing. It was also good to know that Jasleen had someone else in her corner. I said, "So you guys must be pretty close?"

She said, "Very close. She's my sister from another mister."

I laughed. "Well, that's good, cause she could really use a sister right now."

Candice smiled, but the smile slowly disappeared and a look of sadness came over her. She said, "You know what sucks the most? Jasleen was finally back to being herself, and then all of *this* happened."

I said, "What do you mean?"

"Her ex, he just kinda turned her into a different person for a while. She used to be this really free-spirited girl, but that asshole always had a problem with that. And he just slowly changed her into what *he* wanted her to be. That was really hard for me to see. We've been best friends since elementary school and all of a sudden I didn't recognize her anymore. I was always trying to convince her to break up with him, which started causing problems between *us*. But then when he hit her — I mean, I don't wanna say it was a good thing… obviously it wasn't — but at least it finally made her see the light and leave him. And when she did, I swear I was the happiest person in the world. You know that night we met you and your friends? We actually went out that night to celebrate her freedom. And even though she ended up having a little *too* much fun, I was still happy for her." Then she got this embarrassed look on her face and said, "And to be totally honest, when I saw her with you, I was like 'Oh god, just what she needs right now, some random fuckboy all over her.' But I guess you turned out okay."

I smiled and said, "Thanks."

Jasleen finally got off the phone, came back into the kitchen and said, "He's here", which was followed by a knock at the door.

I had an image in my head about what this dude would look like. Clean-cut, handsome, sharply dressed. The 'good guy' you see in movies who always said and did the right thing and was in complete control of his life. Normally pre-conceived notions about a person are proven wrong, but in this case, they couldn't have been more right. He was almost exactly who I thought he would be. And yet, for some reason, I was still surprised. I guess I was thinking, and maybe hoping, he wouldn't live up to my expectations. But he did.

He gave Jasleen a long hug in the doorway, as if to say, "Don't worry, big brother's gonna make everything alright." And judging by the change in Jasleen's demeanor, she really believed he could. After giving Candice a hug too, he extended his hand towards me and said, "Nice to meet you. Harman."

I said, "Indo… nice to meet you too."

As we shook hands, I could feel him judging me while

simultaneously trying *not* to judge me. I figured Jasleen had told him good things about me, but he probably wanted to make up his own mind. I was the guy who knocked up his sister after all.

We all sat down in the living room, except Jasleen, who went into the kitchen to get Harman something to drink. There was an awkward silence until Harman, who was sitting on the couch across from me, made the first attempt at small talk. He said, "So what part of San Jose are you from?"

I said, "Berryessa."

"Oh really? That's where my wife's from."

"Oh… tight."

He looked at me, expecting a follow-up question. What's her name? Which high school did she go to? But I didn't ask a thing, and we went back to the awkwardness until Jasleen returned with a glass of water. Once she took a seat next to me, Harman got down to business. He looked at me and said, "Alright, first of all, my Dad's really sorry for what he did to you yesterday. Obviously, he shouldn't have done that and he knows he was wrong."

I shrugged and said, "All good man. I survived."

Then he turned to Jasleen and said, "I had a long talk with him and he's still pretty upset about everything. But I told you made a mistake and what's done is done, and, you know, we just have to make the best of it now. And it took some convincing, but… he agreed to let you come home."

Right away I could see a sense of cautious relief in Jasleen. But Harman wasn't finished. He said, "The only thing is… you guys gotta get married right away."

Jasleen turned to me to see how I'd react. I tried not to. It wasn't a big surprise to me and it sounded like Harman had more to add, so I let him continue. "And by right away I mean like, within a month or so. People are gonna ask questions about why it's happening so quickly and they're gonna come up with their own theories, but that just kinda is what it is. Like I said, we're trying to make the best out of a bad situation."

He was about to go on when I interrupted and said, "What if we don't wanna get married right away?"

He didn't understand what I meant. "Uhh, you don't really have much of a choice."

I said, "Well, considering *we're* the ones getting married, I think we kinda do have a choice."

"Okay, yeah of course, I don't mean it like that. But the problem is... Jasleen can't be 'showing' during the wedding."

"Alright, then we'll wait till after she has the baby to get married."

Both him and Jasleen looked at me like I was crazy. He said, "Are you joking?"

I shook my head.

He said, "That's not an option."

I said, "What do you mean? It's very much an option. White people do it all the time." I looked over at Candice and said, "Right?"

Candice looked like she wanted no part of the conversation and said, "Umm, yeah. I mean, I don't know about 'all the time', but I guess it happens."

Harman was starting to get fed up with me. He said, "Do we look like white people to you? Listen, I don't think you understand the situation here. My parents are willing to forgive you guys for what you did and move past—"

I cut him off again. "And what did we do exactly?"

"Are you serious?"

I could understand his frustration and confusion. From his perspective, we were criminals and he was our lawyer. He had just spoken to the judge — his Dad — and gotten us the best deal we could have asked for, and I had the audacity to reject it. Jasleen must have saw it that way too. But not me.

I said, "As far as I know, we didn't commit no crime. We didn't kill nobody. So I don't really understand you comin' here and saying we 'have to do this' and 'have to do that'. We don't have to do shit bro. Your parents have to decide whether they wanna be a part of their grandkid's life. So how bout you guys talk that over and let us know?"

Harman was furious. He looked like he wanted to finish the strangling job his Dad never got the chance to. He mustered up as much self-control as he could, and after a long pause, he looked away from me and said, "Can I talk to my sister alone?"

I said, "Of course" and looked over at Candice for some guidance.

She said, "We can go into the bedroom." As I stood up and followed Candice, I could feel Jasleen giving me an angry stare, but I thought it'd be best to avoid making eye contact.

As soon as Candice shut the bedroom door, I said, "Thanks for backing me up bro."

She threw her hands up. "What did you want me to say?"

"*Something* instead of *nothing* would have been nice."

"Oh sure, a white girl giving her 'white girl' opinion. That would've gone over great."

"Really? That's your excuse?"

"It's not an excuse. It's the truth. You know what he

86

would've said if I tried to chime in? 'You wouldn't understand Candice.'"

"You don't know that."

"Trust me, I do. I've been hearing that from Jasleen my whole life."

After a few minutes, we heard the front door close, so we came back out. Jasleen was standing there, alone and upset.

Candice asked, "Where's Harman?"

Jasleen said, "He left."

We were both a little surprised. I said, "He didn't wanna stay for dinner?"

She gave me the angry stare I avoided earlier and said, "What the hell was that?"

"What the hell was what?"

"Why were you being such a dick?"

"Was I?"

"Look, I know you're pissed off about what my Dad did to you, and I totally understand that, but my brother's just trying to help."

"And how's he doing that exactly?"

"Seriously? Were you not paying attention? He convinced my Dad to let me come home!"

"*Let* you come home? You're his daughter. His PREG-NANT daughter... and he kicked you out of the house. What kind of dad would do some shit like that?"

"Well, can you really blame him?

"Yeah, that's what I'm doing."

Jasleen turned to Candice and said, "Can you talk some sense into him please?"

Candice took a deep breath, and as carefully as she could,

said, "Look, I know you don't wanna hear this, but… he kinda has a point."

"Really? You're gonna take his side?"

"It's not about sides. I'm just telling you what I think."

Jasleen rolled her eyes. "Oh my god, you don't understand Candice."

Candice looked at me and said, "See?"

Jasleen said, "See what? What are you talking about?"

"That's what you always say anytime I try to tell you anything."

"Yeah because it's not the same for me as it is for you."

I jumped back in. "Yo, listen… treating your daughter right ain't some 'white people' concept, alright. It's just some shit you're supposed to do."

Candice said, "Thank you. That's all I've been trying to say."

Jasleen didn't wanna hear all that, so she changed the subject. "Do you not wanna marry me?"

I shrugged and casually said, "I don't know."

"What do you mean you don't know? I thought you said you were gonna be *with* me through all this."

"I am. But we also met just a few weeks ago. If we wanna get married someday, we'll do that. But it's gonna be *our* decision, not anybody else's."

She was angry, so of course she didn't listen to anything I said. All she heard was that I was going back on my word. "You know what? If you're having second thoughts about this, you can still back out. It's not too late. I'll just deal with it on my own."

"I never said I wanna back out. I told you before, I'm not

going anywhere. But if we're gonna do this, we gotta do it *my* way."

"What does that even mean?"

"It means you gotta stop acting like you did some horrible thing."

"I fuckin' did!"

"No, you didn't! All you did was make a mistake. But that mistake was yours to make. And nobody has the right to make you feel bad about it — not even your pops. Especially since what he did was a thousand times worse. So, if you ask me, the only way you should go back into that house is if he comes here, apologizes for what he did and BEGS you to come back."

To her that was the most ridiculous thing in the world. She said, "That's fuckin' stupid! It's never gonna happen."

"Well, then you should never go back."

I knew it wasn't gonna be easy to get through to her, but I was hoping my words would at least have *some* effect. Nope. The way she saw it, her Dad's offer was her only chance at re-demption and I had just ruined it. And the fact that Candice was siding with me only made everything worse. Jasleen shook her head in frustration and yelled, "You guys just don't get it!" and stormed off into the bedroom. Me and Candice looked at each other, disappointed and defeated.

Candice said, "Look, she just needs some time, okay. It's a lot to deal with. Just, whatever you do, don't give up on her."

"Yeah, that's not gonna happen. I just hope she doesn't give up on *me*."

"She won't. She's not the type."

I nodded. "Alright, I think I'm gonna get going."

"What?" She gestured towards the kitchen. "What about

the pasta?"

"Yeah, I'm not really that hungry anymore. Sorry."

"Well, take some to go at least."

"Uhh, nah I'm good. Then I'm gonna have to explain to my parents where it came from and all that and it's just… gonna be a whole *thing*."

She sighed. "Alright, fine. Dinner for two then I guess."

I smiled and said, "Three."

It took her a second, but she got it and smiled back. "Oh yeah. Almost forgot."

When I woke up the next morning, I had a missed call from Jasleen. Anytime I had a missed call from her, I'd wait till I was driving somewhere to call her back. In the beginning, I'd call her back right away, but then one day I had a realization — girls like to talk just for the sake of talking. I was always under the impression that a phone call needed to have purpose, and once that purpose was fulfilled, the call would come to an end. But my conversations with Jasleen went on and on. It was pretty much like that with every girl I talked to; I just didn't pick up on it until I met her. So I started using tactics to keep the calls as short as possible. If I knew her school schedule that day, I'd call her back a few minutes before her next class started. If I needed to get to work, I wouldn't call her back until I was on my way there. Things like that. It wasn't that she was a pain in the ass to talk to or anything; she was actually pretty entertaining sometimes. But a dude can only spend so much time on the phone before he starts to lose his mind.

That morning, I broke my own rule and decided to call her back right away. Our argument had been bugging me all night, and I wanted a resolution. Immediately. So I picked up the phone and got ready for round 2. But Jasleen wasn't looking for a fight… she was calling to apologize.

That was the thing about her. She could act like a dick sometimes, but she'd always say 'sorry' as soon as she was back to normal. And when she said it, I knew she meant it. On one hand, that was a good thing, but on the other it was kinda disappointing, because I would spend all this time being angry and looking forward to going off on her, and then I'd never get the chance.

After she apologized, I told her it was okay and that I knew she was under a lot of pressure. I even admitted I was too harsh with her brother. We had a much more civil conversation, but she still didn't get where I was coming from and wanted me to help her understand. So I told her the story about Raveena. From beginning to end. Who she was, what she went through and what she became. And I explained that I didn't want the same thing to happen to *her*, because I knew it would. Because that's what they do to girls like Jasleen and Raveena. First they convince you you're a whore, then they forgive you for being a whore. And you're so grateful for their forgiveness that you feel indebted to them for the rest of your life.

Whenever Jasleen spoke, she spoke with absolute certainty. She didn't leave any room for the possibility that she was wrong. It was kind of annoying actually. Raveena was the exact same way. Both of their birthdays were in August so maybe it was a Leo thing; I don't know. But after listening to Raveena's story, Jasleen asked me question after question, and I heard something in her voice I had never heard before: doubt. Like she was actually considering the idea that maybe she, herself, wasn't so terrible. That maybe what she had done didn't deserve punishment. She didn't let go of all the guilt and shame completely, but she loosened her grip on it just a tiny bit. And that was a start.

Her last question wasn't about Raveena though; it was about me. She said, "Raveena was your cousin, so I can understand why all the stuff that happened to her bothered you so much. But why do you care what happens to *me*? What do you get out of all this?"

It seemed like one of those situations where a girl tries to manipulate you into expressing your feelings about her. But Jasleen had been through a lot, so I felt like she deserved it. I said, "Look, it wasn't that she was related to me. *A lot* of people are related to me. I just really liked Raveena. I felt like she made the world better just by being in it. And then she wasn't 'in it' anymore. And that's what I'm afraid of with you. That by the end of all this… you're not gonna be 'in it' anymore either. So what do I *get* out of all this? I get a world with you in it."

She didn't respond, and after a moment of quiet, I heard sniffling sounds.

I said, "Yo, are you okay?"

She said, "Yeah."

"Are you crying?"

"No."

More sniffling sounds. "Okay, either you're crying or you have allergies all of a sudden. So which is it?"

"It's nothing, I just…"

"What?"

"I don't know… I just… wish you really *were* the father of this baby."

Chapter 11 – A Life Of Its Own

No one *plans* on living a double life. It's not really a thing you set out to do. But sometimes you get yourself mixed up in something so big, it requires a life of its own.

In one life, I was Jasleen's boyfriend and the father of her kid. I was at war with her family, fighting to get her some kind of justice. In the other life, I was my parent's son. A son they used to worry about, but now didn't even bother to question.

Back in the day, my parents didn't really know how I was gonna turn out. I wasn't good in school, I was always getting into trouble, and even though I put in my time at the restaurant, I didn't do it with any enthusiasm. It was just an obligation I had to fulfill. When I went away to college, it gave them some hope that I would make something of myself, but that all came crashing down when I dropped out. At that point, I wanted to do something to earn their trust. They were good parents and I felt like they deserved a good son. I also needed a distraction from all the other stuff going on at the time, so the logical thing for me to do was dedicate myself to the family business.

I guess the time away gave me a different perspective, because as soon as I started working at the restaurant again, it felt different. For one, I realized I was actually good at it. Up until then, I didn't think I was good at *anything*, so it was nice to have a place I could go where I knew what I was doing. Where I was in control. It didn't matter if I was cooking, waiting tables, dealing with vendors, whatever — I did it all with a sense of authority. As a kid, I was always *comfortable* working in the restaurant, but now I felt in *command*. After a while, I even started coming up with ideas about how the place should be run. Everything from what dishes should be on the menu to how we should advertise. Sometimes my parents would listen, sometimes they wouldn't, sometimes we'd argue, but it was cool to just be involved in those conversations. And whether they agreed or disagreed with the things I said, I think my parents were happy that I was taking such an interest in the restaurant. Over the course of a couple years, I went from a failure in their eyes to a responsible, reliable son. And that meant a lot to me.

When all the stuff with Jasleen started up, it actually kinda worked in my favor. Since, according to my parents, I had finally 'straightened out', it was time to start thinking about marriage. So when they noticed I was always on the phone all of a sudden, or that I'd disappear for hours at a time with some vague explanation, they figured I had a girlfriend. They didn't say anything directly, but I'd get funny little comments from them here and there, and I just let them assume what they wanted to assume. No harm in giving them a little hope. But at the same time, I knew everything I had worked so hard for was in danger. If they ever found out the truth — that their son was pretending to be the father of the unborn grandkid of one of the most prominent Punjabi families in all of California — their worlds would get turned upside down. My parents didn't deserve to be disappointed again and the thought of that happening scared me to death.

94

The other person I worried about was Lucky. Me and him did everything together but I had been MIA for a few weeks. Every weekend, he'd invite me to go out and I'd turn him down, which was unheard of for me. I knew it was only a matter of time before he figured out something was up.

One day I was at the restaurant, making jalebis in the deep fryer, when I heard someone behind me exaggeratedly clearing his throat. I turned around, and it was him. I said, "Hey what's up bro?"

Lucky responded in a subdued kind of way. "What's up man?"

"Nothin' much. Same ole thing. Where you comin' from?"

"I was just on my way to work… thought I should stop by."

"Nice, nice."

There was brief, uncomfortable silence, as Lucky stood there watching me. Finally, he said, "So, where you been?"

"Nowhere, just here. Been super busy, you know."

"Too busy for *us*?"

"Nah, it's like I said — we've just had a lot of catering jobs lately, so it's been a little crazy."

"I see."

"Have a jalebi bro." I handed him one. Lucky never turned down a jalebi.

After killing half of it with one bite, he said, "You know what's weird though? I just talked to your Dad out there, and he said you guys haven't really had any more catering jobs than normal."

I was surprised and a little annoyed. "What, you didn't believe me? You had to go verify it?"

He said, "Yeah, and good thing I did. So... what's the deal bruh?"

"Nothing. There ain't no deal."

"You still talking to that chick or what?"

"Uhh, yeah... here and there."

He shook his head. "I knew it."

"Knew what?"

"That night you ditched us to go see her man, I knew that was the end of you."

"Oh god, why you being so dramatic? It ain't like that."

"Okay fine. Then come out with us this weekend."

"I can't."

"Why not?"

"I just can't."

"Your girlfriend won't give you permission?"

That pissed me off. "Or maybe I just don't feel like it. Maybe I'm just sick of doing the same shit every weekend."

"God damn bro. What the fuck did this bitch do to you? Is the head *that* good?"

"Why's it have to be about *her?* I can't just make up my own mind?"

"So it's just a fuckin' coincidence that you had this sudden change at the exact same time you met her?"

"Yes!"

Lucky took a step back and let out a disappointed sigh. "Man, I expected one of those other fools to get pussy-whipped, but I never ever thought it'd happen to you."

"Yeah, okay... you know what you sound like? You sound like a dude who hasn't got none in a while, and it's starting to get to you. And I understand man, it must be hard seeing people around you gettin' some — it must be driving you crazy. But please try to keep it together bro... you don't wanna say some stupid shit and lose a homie for no reason."

I hit a nerve. "Are you fuckin' kidding me? The dude we ain't seen in weeks is telling *me* about losing homies. Mother-fucker we already lost you — I just came here to confirm it."

"Alright, well, if you're done confirming... I got stuff to do, so..."

He said, "Yeah, I'm sure it's probably time for you to check in with your girlfriend, so I'll leave you to it."

I didn't respond, and he took off.

Me and Lucky had arguments here and there, but the cool thing about him was that he had a short memory. We could get into some huge thing, and the next time we saw each other, all was forgotten. He never held a grudge. But this felt different. I knew it was gonna be a long time before things were back to normal between us, and I worried they never *would* be again.

I couldn't really blame him for feeling the way he did though. Me and him had been a tag-team for years and I was breaking us up. More than anything, he was just sad about it. But dudes don't just tell you they're sad — they act like assholes instead.

* * *

Jasleen was approaching the 8-week mark in her pregnancy, and according to her Google searches, that was the about the time you're supposed to get your first check-up. So she made an appointment with her doctor. For the most part, she'd been feeling fine but one of her biggest concerns was the fact that she was drinking the night we met. She didn't know it at the time, but she was already a few weeks pregnant, so it was something she had been really paranoid about.

While we were in the waiting room, I was flipping through some random magazine when Jasleen said, "Remember when we were at the abortion clinic?"

It was a surprising thing for her to bring up. I said, "Yeah" expecting her to say more, but she didn't.

She was quiet for a while, then said, "You know, you never asked me why I didn't go through with it."

I looked at her and said, "I didn't know how to."

She nodded.

"Why didn't you?"

She looked down at the ground. "My Mom had two miscarriages. The first one was before me and Harman were born, but the second one happened way later, when I was nine and Harman was fourteen. I'm pretty sure my parents didn't plan on getting pregnant, but when we found out about it, we were all so excited. Especially me. I always loved babies and now I was gonna get to be this little mini-mom to my new brother or sister. And the closer we got to the due date, the more attached I became to the idea of that.

"Then one day, I woke up and a bunch of my relatives were at my house. Everyone was in this somber mood and at some point, one of my cousins led me to my parents' room. I walked inside and saw my Mom in bed, and my Grandma and a few of my aunts sitting next to her. *They* were all crying, but my

Mom… there was nothing. She just looked empty. There were all these people around her, but it was like she was alone. And she was so far away from me that I got scared she was never coming back.

"On the day of my appointment, all I could think about was how I felt that day when I saw my Mom. And no matter how hard I tried, I couldn't get it out my head."

We went back to quiet for a while. Then I asked, "So do you want me to go inside with you?"

She said, "No, no. They're gonna just do a bunch of tests on me and they might even do a pap smear and… yeah… you can just stay out here."

"Okay, cool."

"Thank you for being here though. It really means a lot."

I let out a laugh. "You don't gotta thank me every five seconds, you know."

She shrugged. "Well I feel guilty every five seconds."

A nurse came out and called her name, and Jasleen got up and followed her to the back. Once they were out of sight, I took out my phone to look up what a pap smear was. After seeing some diagrams, I realized why she didn't want me to come with her.

An hour or so later, Jasleen came out — looking different. As we walked to the car, she told me about all the tests they did and information they gave her, and I could tell by the tone in her voice that the pregnancy had finally become real for her. Not in a positive or a negative way — just in a way that left her no choice but to accept that her life was never gonna be the same.

Most important of all, the doctor said both Jasleen and the

baby were healthy and on the right track. And as far as the concern about the alcohol, she said it was too early in the pregnancy for that to be an issue. Finally, some much-needed good news.

On the way back from the appointment, Jasleen's phone started to ring. She pulled it out of her purse and answered. "Hey... yeah we're driving back now... no, *he's* driving... yeah they said everything looks good, they did all these tests and stuff and kinda walked me through what to expect..." The conversation went on and on, while I listened curiously, wondering who it could be. They talked about the baby, about Jasleen's parents, the anniversary party, and even talked about me for a bit. As I pulled up in front of the apartment building, she finally hung up.

I asked, "Who was that?"

She said, "It was my bhabhi." Her sister-in-law. It was Mahi.

It turned out Jasleen and Mahi were close and had been talking a lot since everything had gone down. When she called Jasleen that day, Mahi and Harman were driving back home after visiting the parents. Mahi said they were distraught and completely at a loss about what to do. When Harman told them what I said, his Dad was outraged. He was sure I would agree to the express marriage idea, and probably even thought I'd be grateful to him for giving me the opportunity. Never in a million years did he think I'd turn him down. But the moment his anger subsided, he must have realized what *I* knew from the beginning — that me and Jasleen had all the leverage in this situation.

I had seen the routine before. First they get angry and make a big scene, then they 'accept' you as if they're doing you a favor. But the reality was, they didn't have a choice. Because even though it looks bad to get your pregnant daughter married in a hurry, it looks much worse to kick her out of your house and let her give birth to your grandkid on the street. That's enough to damage your reputation permanently — and to Punjabi people, reputation means everything.

The way Harman told the story made it sound like I had gotten Jasleen pregnant and was refusing to man up and take responsibility. So, in their eyes, I was the villain in this story. But they were stuck with me. I was the father of their future grandkid, so they had to find a way to come to some sort of understanding with me. And in order to do that, somebody amongst them had to be the voice of reason. And nobody was more qualified than their daughter-in-law.

When we were in high school, me and Mahi had a group of friends. And just like in any group of friends, sometimes shit would happen and people would have issues with each other. *This* person would get into an argument with *that* person, or these two people would stop talking to each other for whatever reason. Normal high school stuff. But nobody ever had an issue or an argument with Mahi. It wasn't possible to. She was too sensible and mature and was always the one *resolving* problems between the rest of us.

When somebody thinks they're right, it's almost impossible to convince them they're wrong, but Mahi had this innocuous way of talking to you, and if she said you messed up, it made you be like, *Man... I guess I messed up.*

And it wasn't just that she was good at making everyone get along... she *needed* everyone to get along. She couldn't handle even the slightest bit of tension between any of us, so she was always desperate to keep the peace. Knowing her, she must have been broken up about everything going on between Jasleen and her parents, and it was only a matter of time before she would try to do something about it.

The phone call to Jasleen was to tell her about a dinner Mahi was arranging where all of us would sit down together and come to an agreement. We accepted the invitation.

Chapter 12 – The Last Time

A few days before the dinner, I was trying to remember the last time me and Mahi were together. The last time I actually saw her was the night before the wedding, but those were just a few brief glimpses. The last time we actually talked was when I came back from Chico, but that was a difficult and awkward conversation. The last time we were really *together* together was all the way back in high school, on the night of the senior prom.

In the months leading up to the prom, she had a dilemma. She really wanted to go but knew her parents wouldn't let her go with anyone but me. This was a problem, because she also knew I wasn't exactly the type of dude who would go to a prom. And on my end, even if I did want to go (and I didn't), I wouldn't have known how to ask her. Our relationship was too weird. Not weird in a bad way; just weird. We didn't know what we were to each other. We definitely weren't boyfriend and girlfriend, but it never felt like we were just friends either. It was something else altogether. When we were kids, we were just kids, so it didn't matter, but when we became teenagers, it started to affect things between us. All of a sudden, we were attracted to each other and didn't know how to process it. If you become attracted to somebody you just met, you more or less know how to move forward, but if it's somebody you've known as long as you've known yourself, what are you supposed to do?

The closer we were getting to the prom, the more she was feeling the pressure from her friends. They were all buying dresses and making arrangements, and she was getting left behind. One day, she came over to my house to drop off some vegetables from her Mom's garden, and as I made room for them in our fridge, she casually brought up the topic. She said, "Oh, the prom's coming up pretty soon."

I said, "Yeah, are you gonna go?

"Nah, my parents would probably trip out about me going with some random guy."

"Yeah, that's true."

There was a short silence, and then she said, "I mean, if it was somebody they knew, then maybe they'd be okay with it."

It wasn't hard to figure out what she was hinting at. But I kept playing dumb. "Is there anybody from school that they know?"

She thought about it for a moment. "No, not really. I mean… besides you."

She set me up perfectly. That was my moment to step in, save the day and be her hero. But for whatever reason, I couldn't bring myself to do it. I let the moment die a slow, painful death.

On the day of the prom, I felt bad. I knew she was sitting at home by herself, probably down and depressed, thinking about all the fun her friends were having. And it was all my fault. So, I figured I should probably do something to make up for it.

The county fair was going on that week. It was a weak substitute for the prom, but it was the best I could come up with, so I called her up and asked if she wanted to go. She wasn't really feeling the idea, but I talked her into it.

On the drive there, she didn't say a single word and I thought to myself, *Man... this is gonna suck. I should've just let her stay at home and cry.*

We got to the fair and did all the things you do at a fair — went on some rides, ate a little cotton candy, played a few games — and she tried her hardest to not have a good time. But the longer we were there, the more she began to enjoy herself. She was very much a kid at heart, so it was only a matter of time before that sour look on her face disappeared. And once it did, she had the time of her life. And so did I.

At the end of the night, we were sitting on the grass watching the fireworks, and I said, "Sorry, you didn't get to go to your prom."

She said, "Oh my god... I totally forgot about all that."

I don't know if she was telling the truth or not, but it made me feel good. And as we sat there watching the fireworks, she put her head on my shoulder — something she had never done before. A lot of girls have touched me in a lot of different ways since then... but nothing has ever compared to that head on my shoulder.

Chapter 13 – The Dinner

As me and Jasleen were driving to her parents' house, a strange thought entered my mind: What if Mahi wasn't who I thought she was? The image of her that I had in my head was created when I was basically a kid. Now, I was an adult. And sometimes things that mean everything to you when you're young, mean nothing to you when you get older. So what if whatever I felt for her was nothing more than a childhood fantasy I outgrew? And what if the moment I saw her... I realized that? What if Mahi wasn't everything I made her out to be?

It was the same drive, up the same hill, to the same house, but the circumstances were a lot different this time. For one, there were no more secrets to reveal. Everything was out in the open — or *almost* everything. We also wouldn't have to deal with the Uncle's family because Mahi purposely planned the dinner on a day when they were gonna be visiting one of their daughters in Fresno.

But the biggest difference of all, was with Jasleen. The last time we were there, she looked at herself as someone who was stigmatized. Someone who had lost her right to have a say in her own life. But now, she was starting to consider the idea that her pregnancy didn't disqualify her from happiness. That maybe she still deserved the chance to live the way she wanted.

When we got to the front door, we rang the bell. It must have been weird for Jasleen. She spent her whole life in that house and now, she was like a guest. An unwelcome guest. Her Mom answered and greeted us warmly. I don't really use the word 'sweet', but if there was a word to describe Jasleen's Mom, *sweet* is what it would be. She looked like she wanted to give Jasleen a hug, but couldn't bring herself to do it, which was sad because Jasleen could've really used one.

Jasleen's Mom took us into the living room, where Harman was waiting. He gave Jasleen a hug, then shook my hand and said, "Good to see you again." Despite all the contention between us the first time we met, he was polite. Like he was making a sincere effort to make things work. After we sat down, he looked at me and said, "Hey sorry I took off without saying anything that day. Just had a long drive ahead of me, so…"

I said, "No worries man."

It was a random thing for him to bring up. I had forgotten all about it, but the fact that he remembered and felt bad enough to mention it surprised me.

In Punjabi, Jasleen's Mom asked, "So what do you guys want to drink? Cha? Soda? Water?"

I said, "I'm good Auntie. Thanks."

Then she looked at Jasleen and said, "What about you?"

Harman laughed, "Come on Mom, why are you being so formal? She can go get it herself."

The Mom said, "Well yeah, of course. I was just, you know…"

Jasleen said, "I'm good Mom, it's okay." And she smiled at

107

Harman like she appreciated his attempt to make her feel at home.

A Punjabi girl's outfit is loud. With all the jewelry and accessories, you can hear it coming from a mile away. All of a sudden, I heard one coming towards us. And the closer it got, the faster my heart pounded in my chest. I took a deep, silent breath.

When Mahi came into the room, she was looking downwards, adjusting something on her outfit, so I saw her face before she saw mine. And as soon as I did, I realized I was right. She really wasn't everything I made her out to be... she was even more.

I thought maybe this whole time, it was just a feeling I had in a dream. But it wasn't a dream after all. Everything I remembered, happened. Everything I felt, was real. And I didn't know whether to be relieved or terrified.

She finally looked up... and saw me sitting next to Jasleen. Her body became still. She looked like she didn't know what world she was in anymore. Before she could even process what was going on, her husband introduced me to her. He said, "This is my wife, Mahi."

And for reasons I'll never completely understand, I said, "Nice to meet you."

I don't know why I said it. I guess in some way I thought it would get her in trouble if I acknowledged that we knew each other. And now, Mahi, who was already in shock that I was standing in front of her, that I was the guy who got her sister-in-law pregnant, had to wonder why I was pretending I didn't know her. She barely managed to get the words out but said, "Nice to meet you too."

Then, Jasleen's Dad unenthusiastically entered the room.

Jasleen stared at him, waiting for him to make eye contact so she could greet him, but he couldn't even bring himself to look at her. He just scanned the room for a moment, then turned to me and said, "Where are your parents?"

When the dinner was being planned, he had asked for them to be there. But I was obviously nowhere near ready to tell 'em about the situation I had gotten myself into. Jasleen understood that, so she made up some excuse about why they couldn't make it. Apparently, no one bothered to tell her Dad because he assumed they were coming, and when he found out they weren't, he wasn't happy. His whole plan was to use my parents to put pressure on me to get married, so to him, there was no point in even *having* this dinner without them there.

I said, "They were busy. They couldn't make it."

He said, "What could be more important than *this*?"

Jasleen's Mom quickly jumped in. In Punjabi, she said, "Sometimes people already have plans. It's okay."

Meanwhile, Mahi was standing there not knowing what to do with herself. She was the one who organized this dinner. *She* was supposed to be the voice of reason. But after seeing me, she could barely open her mouth. And without her guidance, this dinner was bound to be a disaster.

Harman, sensing that everything was falling apart before it even started, suggested we move to the dining table. As everyone started walking over, I said, "Can I use the restroom real quick?"

Harman said, "Yeah, just go down the hall and make a right. It's the second—"

Mahi cut him off. "I... I left my phone in the bedroom... I'll show him."

She walked down the hall, and I followed. As soon as we got far enough away from everyone, she turned around and looked at me like she had a million questions and didn't know which one to ask first. Finally, she desperately asked, "What is going on?"

I said, "I'm not sure."

"Why are you acting like you don't know me?"

"I don't know... I was just... surprised to see you."

"So you didn't know Jasleen was my sister-in-law?"

"No, no... I swear."

She was trying hard to make the reality of the situation sink in, but it just wasn't happening for her. After a while, she gave up, pointed to a door and said, "The bathroom's right there," and quickly walked away.

We all sat down at the dinner table. A bunch of fancy silver bowls were laid out in the center, each with a different color dish. Rice, gobi, daal, chicken, raitha — Jasleen's Mom must have spent all day cooking.

The tension was thick as we started eating, and for the longest time, all you could hear was the sounds of silverware clinking. Eventually, Jasleen's Dad broke the silence. In Punjabi, and without looking up, he said, "So what did you guys decide?"

Now it was Jasleen's time to speak. She put down her fork, looked at me, then looked at her Dad and said, "Dad... I'm sorry this happened. I know I made a mistake. But after seeing what this mistake did to my life, and how much pain it caused everyone I care about... I can't take a chance on making another one. Before I get married, I wanna make sure I'm ready, and right now... I'm not."

He said, "Why aren't you ready?"

"Because we've only known each other for a couple months."

He shouted, "Well that didn't stop you from—" He didn't finish the sentence, and didn't need to. He continued, "No, of course not. Because when it came to that, you were only thinking about *yourself.* And now, when it comes to doing something for your *family*, all of a sudden you want to think about things and be careful?"

Jasleen didn't answer the question. She couldn't. All it took was one angry outburst and she was scared into submission. It was a disturbing thing to witness. Jasleen wasn't some shy or timid girl — if anything, she was the complete opposite. But in front of her Dad, all that went away. It was like he had some kind of mind control over her. And that, combined with the shame of being an unwed, pregnant Punjabi girl, was too much for her to overcome. It didn't matter how many lectures I gave her, and I gave her a lot; in the end she had to stand up to him on her own. And she couldn't.

Her Dad continued, "Look, enough of your nonsense. Just listen to what we're saying. We know what's best for you."

This is where Mahi would've jumped in and brought some calm to the conversation, but she was in no condition to do that. I guess Harman and his Mom didn't want to give the impression they were siding with Jasleen, so they kept quiet too. That left it up to me.

After waiting a moment to see if anyone else would say anything, I looked at Jasleen's Dad and said, "Uncle ji, if Jasleen wasn't pregnant and she came to you and said, 'Dad, there's this guy I've known for 2 months and I wanna marry him. And not just that... I wanna marry him next week.' What would you say?

Would you be okay with it?"

Harman got a sense of where I was going and wasn't happy about it. It was obvious he never talked back to his Dad and didn't approve of anyone else doing it either. Just as he was about to say something, his Dad decided to humor me. "No, of course I wouldn't."

I said, "Okay, then how is it you throw a baby into that situation and it all of a sudden becomes a good idea?"

"Who said it's a good idea? Do you think we *want* to do this? That we're doing it happily? We're only doing it because we don't have any other choice."

"Why don't you have a choice? What's gonna happen if this baby is born and we're not married?"

Jasleen's Mom almost gasped at what I was suggesting. It was so outrageous, Jasleen's Dad had to take a second to make sure he heard correctly. He said, "You're Punjabi, right?"

I said, "I think so."

"Well then you should know — that's not how it works. That's not how we do things."

Every time he said something, Jasleen flinched slightly. And every flinch added fuel to my fire. I said, "That's not what I'm asking you. I'm asking you what exactly is gonna *happen*."

Mahi was looking down at her plate the entire time, like this was all a bad dream and she was just waiting to wake up.

Jasleen's Dad started to get impatient. He looked around at everyone, then back at me and said, "Are you stupid or just pretending to be stupid? You don't know what's gonna happen to our reputation? You don't know what people are gonna say about us?"

And there it was. All roads lead back to those *people*, and what they're gonna say. I swear if I had any enemies in the world, it was them. And what always bothered me more than anything was just how few of *them* there really were. Because the truth is, most people don't sit around and talk about other people's problems. Even if they wanted to, they wouldn't have the time. It's only the ones whose lives are the most empty. The ones who have the least to give, always have the most to say.

I said, "That's it? No jail time? No fines we gotta pay? Some 'people' are just gonna 'say' some stuff? I hope you have a better reason than *that*."

Every word that came out of my mouth made the veins in his head get bigger. And everyone at the table was bracing themselves for him to explode. But he just sat there quietly, so I continued, "And who are these people? Do we get to meet them? I mean, if they're gonna decide when and how we get married, I think we should at least get to meet them. So how about we do this? We'll compromise. If you can call all these 'people' over here, and we can see them face to face and hear what they have to say, then we'll get married whenever you want, wherever you want, however you want. Does that work for you?"

He gave me a long, intense stare, then shook his head. Then, in Punjabi, he said, "You kids these days are so smart. You have everything figured out. 'Who cares what people think? What does it matter to us? Let's just live our lives however we want to.'" He leaned forward onto the table. "Let me explain to you how things *really* work. We all live in a community. And in that community, there's a way of doing things. There are things you do, and there are things you *don't* do. And if you do things the wrong way, you lose respect. And respect means everything to us. Our whole community is built on respect. Tell me something… have you ever seen a Punjabi person living on the street? Or Punjabi grandparents living in a nursing home? You haven't, right? If your house burned down tomorrow, would you have a place to go? You would, right? You have all kinds of relatives and friends who would gladly take you in for as long as you need. Do you know why that is? Because in this community, we take care of each other. We look out for each other. But that wouldn't be possible if we all just said, 'Who cares what people think?' That's something other people say… and look at all the problems they have. But us, we *do* care. Because that's how we show respect to our community… and that's what keeps us strong."

There was a lot of truth in what he was saying. But it wasn't the whole truth. Nobody ever tells the whole truth.

I said, "Uncle ji… so… when you choked the father of your future grandkid… was that about respect too? Or what about when you kicked your pregnant daughter out of your house? What was that? If those are the kinds of things that get you respect in this community… then I think we'll be fine without it."

He finally lost it. "What part of this don't you understand? You can't have this baby without getting married!"

I said, "Actually I'm pretty sure we can. I don't think the baby's gonna ask for a marriage certificate before coming out."

He slammed his fist on the table. "It's no use talking to you! That's why I told you to bring your parents!"

"Well, see the thing is — the last time I was in this house, someone attacked me. So I wasn't sure if it'd be safe to bring my parents into this kind of environment."

Maybe I went too far, because he immediately stood up and yelled, "What is that supposed to mean?"

I didn't answer. Harman got up and tried to calm him down. "Dad, it's okay."

He said, "No, it's not okay! You think I would attack your parents?"

I shrugged. "Who knows?"

I had never seen someone so angry. I was sure he was gonna leap across the table at any moment and beat the life out of me. But that would've just proven my point, and I think he realized that. So instead, he stormed off. And that was the end of the dinner.

Harman looked at me with disgust and said, "What the hell is your problem man?!"

I didn't answer. He was about to continue but he was more concerned about his Dad and decided to go after him. Everyone else at the table was shaken. Jasleen's Mom turned to me with desperation in her eyes, and in Punjabi said, "Look son, you have to understand how hard this is for us. I know what you're saying — it shouldn't matter what people say... but it does, and we have to think about these things."

She was a lot harder to argue with and I made sure to give some thought to how I'd respond. Finally, with as soft a tone as I could use, I said, "Auntie ji, I know it's not easy for you guys, and I promise I'm not trying to make it harder. I know we made a mistake." Then I pointed at Jasleen's stomach. "But that's our kid, and your grandkid. And someday that kid's gonna grow up and ask questions. And I wanna be able to tell him or her, that even though it was a crazy time when we found out you were on your way... I was never ashamed of you. Don't you wanna be able to say the same thing?"

She thought long and hard about my question, but what kind of answer could she really give me? She was in a no-win situation. I looked at Jasleen, who was still silent, and said, "We should probably get going."

Everyone got up and said their goodbyes. Mahi gave Jasleen a hug, then looked at me and said, "It was nice meeting you."

The shock wasn't even close to wearing off. I tried to apologize with my eyes and said, "It was nice meeting you too."

That night, I was expecting Mahi to call or text me and ask for an explanation. I sat up in my bed, staring at my phone, waiting for it to make a sound. But it never did. Maybe she was expecting *me* to be the one to reach out to explain. I don't know. With me and her, there were always too many maybes and never enough no's and yes's.

Chapter 14 – Sex and Violence

There's an age-old, deep-rooted relationship between Punjabis and violence. I don't know how or why it all started; I just know it goes back a long way and continues to this day. It's a part of the culture. There's violence at our celebrations, there's violence at our shows, there's even violence in our temples. It's our problem-solving method of choice. If you're Punjabi, chances are you've either used violence to solve a problem you had with someone… or someone used it to try to solve a problem they had with *you*. Up until then, I had been lucky enough to not have experienced either situation. But sooner or later, everyone's luck runs out.

Candice had gone out of town for the weekend, so Jasleen was at the apartment alone. A few days after the dinner, pregnancy sickness started kicking in and she was throwing up like crazy. She asked me if I could spend the night with her and I said, "Cool."

I had to work that day, but on my way to the restaurant, I stopped by the apartment to check on her and drop off some ginger and lemons she asked me to pick up from the store. There was a question I had wanted to ask her since the day I found out she was pregnant, but I wasn't sure how to ask it. And for whatever reason, I picked that day to give it a shot.

When I got there, she was laying on the couch, under a blanket, watching TV. I said, "Damn… that bad?"

She said, "No, a lot better than last night. Just hella tired cause I couldn't sleep." I put the grocery bag on the dining table and she said, "Thanks."

"So what's all that for?"

"Lemon ginger tea."

"Oh. Is that supposed to help?"

"No, it's supposed to make it worse."

I rolled my eyes.

She gave me her fake evil laugh, then smiled and said, "I don't know. My bhabhi said I should try it."

I nodded.

"So what'd you think of her by the way?"

"Huh? Uhhh, I don't know… she seemed nice."

"Yeah, she is."

I looked towards the door.

She said, "You gotta go?"

I said, "Uhh, nah. I can chill for a bit," and sat down next to her on the couch. "What are you watching?"

"Days of Our Lives."

"What's that?"

"A soap opera. Me and my Mom used to watch it together."

We watched the show, while I thought of the right way to bring up my question. A few minutes into it, two of the characters started making out, and Jasleen immediately changed the channel. I said, "What happened?"

She said, "Shit, sorry, it's just a reflex." She changed it back. "Whenever there was a kissing scene my Mom would yell at me to change the channel."

I laughed.

We continued watching, until I finally decided to throw it out there. I said, "Yo, so uhh... I was gonna ask you something."

She said, "Yeah?"

"Uhh..." Then I thought twice about it and said, "Actually, never mind."

"What?"

"Nothing. It's kind of a weird question."

She turned down the volume, sat up straight and turned towards me. "I don't mind weird questions."

I hesitated for a moment or two, then said, "Alright... so... check it out. I was just wondering... if your boyfriend was such a bad guy, right? And your relationship was such a bad relationship... and you knew it was coming to an end... why did you still..."

I didn't finish the sentence hoping she would figure out what I was asking. It took her a second, but she did, and immediately got defensive. "I don't know, it just kinda happened."

She was hoping the vague answer would make me let the topic go, but I wasn't ready to. I said, "Yeah, but I mean, if he was such an asshole, how could you bring yourself to do that with him?"

That got under her skin. She said, "Are you trying to say this whole thing was my fault?"

"No. I'm just trying to figure out how it happened."

"I don't know. It was stupid. I guess I'm just stupid!"

"If you were stupid, I wouldn't be asking you this question. I would already know the answer. What I'm trying to wrap my head around is how a smart girl like you could put herself in that situation. That don't make any sense to me."

"It doesn't make any sense to me either, alright. And I've spent every day since then regretting it, so thanks for giving me another reminder of how bad I fucked up."

I closed my eyes and shook my head. "You know what, never mind. This is why I didn't wanna ask you in the first place — cause you can't answer a simple fuckin' question without losing your shit."

"Yeah well that's kind of a messed up question to ask someone."

"No it ain't, it's just me trying to understand something I don't understand… that's all."

"What's there to understand? We were together, I was horny and things happened."

All of a sudden, she froze up, as if the words that came out of her mouth surprised her.

I said, "Wait, what?"

She didn't answer. Her whole demeanor changed and she went into her own thoughts.

I said, "That's it?"

She looked up at me and slowly nodded.

"You fucked him because you were horny? That's the reason all this happened?"

It was hard for her to admit it, but she was making a conscious effort to be honest with me and herself. She said, "Yes."

I was so disappointed in her answer that I almost lost a little bit of respect for her. I said, "You couldn't just control yourself?"

Looking back at it, I'm surprised she didn't get offended by my judgmental-ass tone. But I guess she was too busy processing her own realization to pay attention to the way I was talking. She said, "I guess not."

I said, "How is that possible?"

"I don't know."

I shook my head. "Look... you gotta give me some better explanation than *that.*"

She said, "Well, I mean... what if *you* were in the same situation? What if you were in a relationship for a long time, it went bad, and you were trying to get out? But one night you were with this girl and you had desires that needed to be fulfilled. Could you imagine yourself losing control?"

I gave it some thought and said, "Yeah... I can. But that's different."

She said, "Why? Because you're a guy?

"Uhhh, yeah."

She raised her eyebrows at me and said, "You do know that girls get horny too, right?"

"Yeah, obviously."

"No, I mean like, just as horny as guys do."

"Woah, woah, wait. Look I know girls get horny and all that, I'm not stupid, but it ain't nowhere *close* to how horny *we* get, okay. You have no idea."

She said, "No, *you* have no idea. There are times when I don't just want it, I *need* it. Like it's all I can think about, and it feels like my body's on fire. Have you ever felt like *that* before?"

"Uhh... well... maybe not to that extent, but—"

"Okay then talk to me when you have."

"Alright hold up, but... then why do y'all always act like you don't want to and stuff?"

"Because we *have* to act like that. It's just the way it is. There's so many things girls have to think about that you guys don't. So we pretend."

"Okay but you can't be *that* good at pretending."

"Uhh, we kinda *are*. You remember the first time we hung out? In your car?"

"Yeah."

"The way I was feeling that night, if it wasn't for all those million things we have to take into consideration... I would've been all over you within the first five minutes."

I was speechless for a moment. "For real?"

She nodded.

I took a second to let that sink in, then said, "Damn... if only I would've known that."

She stared at me and said, "Well... you know it *now*."

Somewhere along the way, the look in her eyes changed. And so did the look in mine. All of a sudden, forces beyond our control started slowly pushing us closer together.

Every time that had happened before, someone got in the way. The first time, it was Jasleen's friend. The second time, it was the cop. This time... it was Mahi. Just as we were about to kiss, the thought of her came into my mind, and I stopped myself. In a weird panic, I looked towards the clock on the wall and said, "I should probably get to work. I'm getting late."

She was confused. "Oh... okay."

I stood up. "But yeah, I'll see you tonight. Let me know if you need me to pick up anything else from the store or whatever."

"Uhh, sure, I will. Thanks."

She was a little jarred by my change in demeanor, so to make things less awkward, I said, "We'll continue this conversation when I get back." She nodded, skeptically, as I walked out the door.

That night was one of the busiest nights we've ever had at the restaurant. Gurdas Mann, a famous Punjabi singer, was having a concert at the Civic Center in downtown, so a ton of people were coming through to have dinner before the show. And since there was a thunderstorm going on outside, every one of their fancy outfits was rain-soaked.

I was mostly in the kitchen, running around, trying to keep up with the orders. At a certain point, one of the waiters, Karim, came to me and said there was a group of guys refusing to pay their bill. They were claiming to be family. I figured it was probably some of my Dad's friends trying to get a free meal, so I looked through the window into the dining area and asked Karim to point them out. All the way back at a booth in the far corner, were a group of young Punjabi guys. One of them was Satti, Jasleen's mean-mugging, shit-talking cousin. Fuck.

My Dad was in the back, loading up the truck for a catering job, and I hoped to god he would stay busy long enough for me to handle the situation. I went out there with Karim and walked over to their table. As soon as Satti saw me, he put on a fake smile and said, "Hey what's up bro? Good to see you again."

I smiled back and said, "What's up man? You finally made it out."

"Yeah, I told you I would."

"Yes you did. But hey, uhh... my boy Karim here tells me you don't wanna pay the bill. Was there something wrong with the food?"

"Oh no, not at all. The food was amazing. But you know, we figured that since we're family now, you'd probably be insulted if we tried to pay for it."

This motherfucker. Now I had to find a way to make him

123

pay his bill without causing a scene. After thinking about it for a moment or two, I thought of a better solution. "You know what bro? You're right, we *are* family. Consider your dinner on the house. You guys have a good night."

As I started to walk away, he said, "Woah, hold on man. What's the rush? Why don't you sit down and join us? We were thinking about getting some drinks. I mean, if it's okay with you."

"Yeah, that's fine man. Go ahead and order whatever you want. Karim will get it for you... but me, I actually gotta get back to the kitchen."

"Well if you're too busy, maybe you can send your Dad out here and *he* can have a drink with us."

Satti was trying to figure out if my Dad knew anything about the Jasleen situation, and even though I didn't say anything, I think my reaction gave it away. He looked at Karim, and said, "Can we get five glasses of Blue Label on the rocks?" Then he turned to me. "You okay with that?"

I nodded reluctantly and indicated to Karim that he should go ahead and get the drinks. Then, I sat down, looked at Satti and said, "I'm sorry bro, I forgot your name. What was it again?"

Satti leaned forward. "Don't worry about what my name is, bitch." The friendly act was over. "Lemme ask you something... do you wanna get your ass beat in your own restaurant, in front of your customers?"

He waited for me to respond, but I didn't.

He said, "Yo, I'm talking to you."

I said, "Oh, sorry, I thought it was a rhetorical question."

Satti looked at his boys. "This fool got jokes." He turned back to me. "You think I'm fuckin' playing with you boy?"

"I don't know *what* you're doin' bro."

"Alright then lemme make this shit real simple for you. You're gonna go to my Chacha [uncle] and tell'em you're ready to get married. Then you're gonna get together with your family, and y'all are gonna start making wedding plans. Is that easy enough for you to understand?"

They had me by the balls. In one move, they could expose me to my parents, damage our restaurant's reputation, and smash my face in. And there wasn't much I could do about it. Knowing all that, I should have just agreed to do what he said for the time being and figured out the rest later. But a guy can be his own worst enemy sometimes. I looked at Satti and said, "Yeah, I think I get what you're saying man."

He said, "Good."

"But see, here's the thing — how can I make wedding plans if your cousin hasn't even proposed to me yet? Doesn't a guy at least deserve that much?"

His eyes got wide. "You wanna find out what your punk ass deserves? Cause I can show you right now."

One more wrong answer is all it would've taken to push him over the edge. But before I could open my mouth again... Lucky walked into the restaurant.

I couldn't believe it. It was like he was sent there to save me from myself. And as soon as he spotted me, he must have somehow sensed I was in trouble, because he walked right over and started aggressively introducing himself to everyone at the table. Then he looked at Satti and asked, "Is it cool if I join you guys?"

Lucky's sudden appearance threw Satti off, and it took him a second to regain his composure. Finally, he said, "Uhh... well, actually man, we were kinda in the middle of something."

Lucky said, "Oh yeah? Middle of what?"

"Nothing… we're just trying to settle a little disagreement we had."

"Oh, well, you're in luck bro, because I'm really good at settling disagreements." Lucky sat down across the table from Satti without letting him say another word.

Satti must have figured I called for backup, and he wasn't pleased about it. He sat there for a moment, studying Lucky's face, while Karim came back with the drinks and placed them on the table. He even brought an extra one for Lucky.

Lucky said, "So what's the problem? Maybe I can help."

Satti looked around at his boys, then at me, then back at Lucky and said, "You know what man? Maybe you *can* help." He leaned forward again. "Let's just say… you had a little sister—"

Lucky cut him off. "We don't have to just say it bro, I *do* have a little sister."

"Oh, perfect. Then this should be easy for you to understand. I'm sure you really care about your little sister, right?"

"Of course. What kinda brother wouldn't?"

"Exactly. So now, just imagine real quick, that your little sister met a guy. A guy she really liked. And after the two of them got to know each other better, she started trusting this guy. And she trusted him so much, that one day… she got a little carried away, and let things go too far. But this guy, I guess he didn't really believe in being careful, because your little sister… she ended up getting pregnant. But instead of manning up and taking responsibility… this motherfucker refused to marry her. Now let's say all that happened to your little sister. Your little sister that you love and you care about and you're supposed to protect. What would you do about it?"

Knowing everything I knew about Lucky, I was sure his jaw was gonna drop. Lucky was very much about tradition, and the culture, and all those kinds of things, so I was even halfway expecting him to say, "Wait, what?! Is *that* what he did? Well, in that case, I'll leave you guys to it." But he didn't even have bat an eyelash. He took a moment, gave it some thought, then looked at Satti and said, "You know what I would do?" He paused to take a sip of his drink. "I would slap the shit outta my sister for getting involved with a piece of shit like that in the first place."

Everyone was a little taken aback. Satti said, "And what about the piece of shit himself?"

Lucky shrugged. "What about'em?"

"*What about'em?* Are you for real? Look homie, I don't know what kinda family *y'all* got, but in mine we look out for our women. We don't let no punk motherfuckers take advantage of'em and walk away."

I re-entered the conversation. "I didn't say nothin' about walking away."

"I don't give a fuck to what you said. Actions speak louder than words bro. If you're not trying to marry my cousin, it means you're trying to find a way out. It's as simple as that".

Lucky said, "Yo, if this guy really knocked up your cousin, then I can tell you he ain't the type to walk away. So if you're not gonna take *his* word for it, you can take mine."

Satti wasn't impressed. "I don't need your word *or* his word. Words don't mean shit! All I need is for you to talk some sense into your boy, otherwise we're about to have a problem."

"Look, just chill the fuck out man."

"No, you chill out!" The other customers started noticing the commotion and I could feel more and more eyes on us. Satti turned back to me. "I'm gonna ask you one last time — you gonna marry my cousin or not?"

I said, "Not till I get my ring."

"Motherfucker! You think this is funny?!"

Lucky said, "Yo, keep your voice down."

"Man, fuck you!"

"Look, I'm asking you nicely."

"I don't give a fuck! What are you gonna do about it?"

Lucky paused for a moment... then pulled back one side of his jacket to reveal a gun in a holster. He repeated himself. "Keep your voice down."

Everyone, including me, fell silent. Satti was obviously spooked, but he tried his hardest to play it off. He said, "Oh, that's how it's gonna be huh?"

Lucky said, "That's not how I *want* it to be, but that's how I can make it be."

"You just made a big ass mistake bro. You know who the fuck I am?"

"Nah man, I don't know who you are. But now you know who *I* am... so keep that shit in mind before you come around here again."

Satti started nodding aggressively. "Alright, alright... y'all wanna take it *there*? We can take it there too." Then he stood up and looked down at me. "Just watch yourself from now on bruh... that's all I gotta say."

He headed for the exit, and his boys got up and followed. As soon as they were out the door, I let out a heavy breath. Lucky finally turned towards me. He hadn't looked at me since he sat down. But I wasn't quite ready to make eye contact yet, so I stood up and said, "Put that shit away bro."

We had this room in the back where we did all the paperwork. It was barely bigger than a closet, but it was the only place you could get some privacy. I led Lucky in there, shut the door, and waited for him to unload.

It took him a little while to figure out where to start, but finally he said, "So is it true? I'm about to be a chacha [uncle]?"

I said, "Uhh... not quite."

"What does that mean?"

"What are you doing here by the way?"

"Karim called me cause he thought some shit was about to go down."

"Oh shit, really? Fuckin Karim man. Need to give that dude a raise."

"Stop changing the fuckin' subject. What the hell's goin' on? I'm guessing he was talking about that same chick?"

I nodded, slowly.

"Fool you never heard of condoms?"

"It ain't what you think."

"What is it then?"

"She was already pregnant when I met'er... she just didn't know it."

His eyes got wide. "Oh... oh shit."

"Her ex-boyfriend is the father. And he's kind of a piece of shit, so when she found out, she didn't wanna tell'em. So... I decided to... pretend the kid was mine."

It took him a moment to wrap his head around what I said. "Excuse me?!"

I nodded.

"What the fuck is wrong with you?"

I shrugged. "I wanted to help her out."

"No, driving someone to the airport is helping them out. This is some other shit altogether. So I hope you got a better explanation."

"I don't know man... it was just something I did. And then I met her family, and they wanted us to get married... and I told 'em we weren't ready for all that. And now, they're kinda not happy about that."

"Well, no shit! They're fuckin' Punjabi, what do you expect? They're not just gonna say, 'Yeah, sure, take your time guys, no rush.'"

"Well that's what they *should* say."

"But they ain't gonna!" Then he paused for a moment, and said "Wait a minute, wait a minute... is *that* what this is about? Are you trying to make one of your fuckin' *points*?"

"What are you talkin' about?"

"You *know* what I'm talkin' about. One of your anti-everything, stupid ass points."

"For real? You think I would do all this just to make a point?"

"Uhh yes, I do. Unless you can give me a different reason."

I couldn't.

He continued, "Look man, it's one thing to have an argument with *me* or your parents or whoever — but this is real life bro. It ain't a joke. What are you fuckin' thinking?"

The door opened. It was my Dad. In Punjabi, he said, "We have a line out the door and you're hiding in here?"

I said, "We were just talking about something real quick, I'll be out in a second."

He sensed something was off and turned to Lucky who quickly put on a smile and said, "Sat Sri Akal, Massar [uncle]."

My Dad responded, "Sat Sri Akal. You wanna help out too? I got an extra apron just for you."

"Oh, sorry Massar, I actually gotta get going. The concert's about to start."

"Okay then hurry up and get going… stop bothering my employees." Then he turned back to me and said, "Come on."

I said, "Alright, I'll be there."

As he closed the door, Lucky got up. "Alright, I'm gonna bounce, but we're gonna continue this conversation." Then he opened his jacket and pulled out the gun. "In the meantime, do me a favor — hold onto this."

"I don't need that man."

"Yo, those dudes weren't messing around. Just take it."

"I don't even know how to use it."

"You don't have to use it… it's just to scare them away."

"Look bro, thank you for coming through and saving my ass. I really really appreciate it. But you know there's no way I'm taking that."

Lucky knew it was no use pushing it, so he put the gun away. "Okay, but listen… when those fools come back, whether it's tonight or tomorrow or whenever — they're gonna come back hard. So make sure you call me when they do."

"Yeah, sounds good."

He took a couple steps towards the door, then stopped. "Oh and by the way, don't tell Navi I said I'd slap the shit out of her."

I said, "Oh, I'm gonna tell'er that for sure. Then we'll see how much of a tough guy you really are."

He laughed as he headed out.

For the next few hours, I was on edge. I knew that at any moment, Satti and his boys could come back, and if they did, it was gonna be for more than just a conversation. I kept one eye out the window for the rest of the night, looking at every car and every person that passed by. They might have been miles away, but to me, they were always just outside the door.

As it got closer to closing time, the place started to empty out. Once all the customers left, the waiters and cooks all went home too. Eventually it was just me and my Dad cleaning up. He was in the kitchen and I was in the dining area, stacking chairs. The rain finally stopped, and it felt like a sign that we were out of trouble.

Then a big pickup truck pulled up outside, shining its high beams through the window. I stopped what I was doing and just stood there, staring at it. Our windows were tinted and I had turned our lights off, so I knew they couldn't see me, but the high beams made it so I couldn't see *them* either. My Dad was still in the back, and I decided to hold off on saying anything to him until I absolutely had to.

Minutes passed and nothing was happening. It seemed like they were waiting for me to come out, so I figured all I had to do was wait it out until they realized no one was inside, and then they'd take off. Another few minutes passed and still no movement. I could tell by the noises in the kitchen that my Dad was wrapping up and I started thinking about what I would say to him. How could I possibly explain?

It turned out I didn't have to because the truck finally started backing up. I breathed a sigh of relief. It turned sideways so that the driver's side door was facing the window, but then, for some reason, it stopped. In my head I was like, *Take off*

132

already motherfucker. What are you waiting for? But the truck wouldn't move.

Suddenly, the driver's side window rolled down and I saw a face covered in a shadow. And then... I saw the barrel of a shotgun. At that exact moment, my Dad came out of the kitchen and I turned towards him and yelled, "Dad! Get on the ground!" I rushed over and tackled him as we heard "Boom! Boom! Boom!" Each gunshot was followed by the sound of shattering glass. After a few seconds of silence, we heard the truck peel out.

When we finally got up, we saw tiny bits of glass everywhere. Some on the floor, some on the tables, and some still in place, trying their best to keep some semblance of a window together. My Dad, shaken and breathing heavily, looked at me and asked, "Are you okay?"

I said, "Yeah... you?"

He nodded.

We walked over to take a closer look at the damage. I put my hand through the giant hole in one of the windows and felt the wind breeze through my fingers. My Dad bent down to pick up a piece of the glass, his hands trembling, then looked up at me and, in Punjabi said, "Who *was* that?"

I took a deep breath, stared him in the eyes and said, "I don't know."

He didn't believe me. "Are you sure you don't know?"

"Yeah... I have no idea."

"What were you and Lucky talking about earlier?"

"Oh, that? No, no, that was about some other stuff."

He gave me another long look. "Listen, if you guys are in trouble, you need to tell me right now."

"No Dad. Come on. If we were, I would tell you. Especially after this. But there's nothing going on I swear. I really don't know who did this."

When the cops asked me the same question, I gave them the same answer. Despite everything that happened, I still couldn't bring myself to let my parents know the truth. I knew it would be too much for them to handle.

Once the cops were gone and the place was boarded up, I looked at my phone and saw a bunch of texts and missed calls from Jasleen. I forgot I was supposed to spend the night with her. By then, I didn't have it in me to talk to or even look at anyone. All I wanted to do was go home. To be in a place that was familiar and still whole. And to think long and hard about what the hell I had gotten myself into.

Chapter 15 - Liberation

A phone call from Jasleen woke me up the next morning. I picked up. "Hello."

In a panic, she said, "Hey, are you okay?"

"Uhh, yeah.

"What happened last night?"

"Nothing, just… can I call you later?"

"Uhh, I guess, but everything's okay right?"

"Yeah, kinda."

"What does that mean?"

"I don't know… lemme just… I'll call you later."

"Alright… fine."

Still wasn't ready. I couldn't get the image out of my head. Those windows had been there since I was a kid, and as far as I knew, they had been there since the beginning of time. So I just assumed they'd be there till the end of it. But in the blink of an eye, they were in pieces on the floor. I couldn't get over how fragile they turned out to be. I tried telling myself that it could've been worse, that it was just windows, but it wasn't really about how *much* got destroyed… it was how *little* it took to destroy it. When I got home, our home didn't even feel like a home to me anymore. It just felt like walls and a roof. And all I could think about was how easily all that could come crumbling down too. How easily there could be *nothing* where there had always been *something*.

After finally getting out of bed and taking a shower, I went into the kitchen. As soon as she saw me, my Mom started crying. She rushed over to give me a hug, and I smiled. "Hey come on, what's all this? I'm fine."

In Punjabi, she said, "You're fine because you were lucky. What if you or your Dad were standing by the window? What if those people came inside? What if—"

I said, "Okay, but we *weren't*... and they *didn't*. So let's not think about all that. Let's just be grateful."

She looked up at me. "Are you okay?"

I put on an even bigger smile. "Yeah, I'm good. I mean, it was little scary... but it's over now."

I tried to downplay it as much as I could, but a mom is a mom, and I think she sensed I was putting on an act. She asked a few more times, but when I kept giving her the same answer, she decided to let me keep acting. As long as I was safe, that was all that mattered to her.

If you have good parents, you don't get a lot of chances to realize how lucky you are. As soon as you learn to walk, you forget about 'em and they settle into the background of your life. But while you're off trying to fulfill your every *want*, they're busy fulfilling your every *need*. And if you ever end up doing anything meaningful, it's not because you *chose* to, it's because they gave you a *chance* to.

My Mom made me aloo parathas for breakfast, and as I was

sitting at the table, eating, she kept looking over at me. It was like she needed constant reassurance that I was still in one piece. After finishing up, I went over and grabbed my keys. She said, "Where you going?"

"Uhh, I just gotta go meet up with Lucky for a little bit."

"No, no, just stay home. Or tell him to come here."

"Oh my god, why?"

"Those people could be looking for you."

"What people?"

She gave me a long stare. "Okay listen. I know what you told your Dad... but are you sure you don't know who they were?"

I sighed. "Yes."

"Do you swear on my life?"

Even though I didn't believe in any of that kinda stuff, I didn't wanna take a chance on putting another one of my parents lives in danger, so I sidestepped the question.

I said, "Mom, I don't have any enemies. You have nothing to worry about, okay. It was just a random thing, done by random, crazy people."

She finally let me off the hook, but just as I was about to leave the kitchen, she said, "Are you really going to see Lucky? Or are you going to see someone else?"

I said, "Someone else like who?"

"Whoever you're always on the phone with."

"Uhh, I'm always on the phone with Lucky."

She smiled. "Okay... then tell 'Lucky' I said hi."

"Bye Mom."

Instead of calling Jasleen back, I decided to just go to the apartment. When I got there, she was on the couch, almost like she hadn't moved since I left the day before. As soon as I walked in, she stood up. She seemed happy that I was okay, but also seemed *not* happy that I was okay.

She said, "I swear to god, you better have a good explanation."

I sat down on the couch across from her without saying anything.

She continued, "You know how fuckin' freaked out I got when I woke up and you weren't there? Do you have any idea? Like, regardless of what was going on, you couldn't just take two seconds to text me that you weren't coming?"

I didn't answer.

"Hellooo… are you listening to what I'm saying?"

"Yeah."

"Okay then, are you gonna respond or are you just gonna sit there?"

I was quiet for another few moments, then asked, "How are you feeling?"

"Uhh, better."

"That's good."

"Alright, now you're starting to weird me out. Can you just tell me what the hell happened last night?"

"Your cousin Satti shot up our restaurant."

She gasped. "What? What do you mean shot up?"

I told her what happened. Satti and his boys. The shit-talking and the threats. Lucky showing up. The pickup truck. The shotgun blasts.

Jasleen put her hand over her mouth and couldn't bring herself to speak for a moment. Finally, she said, "Oh my god. Are you okay? Is your Dad okay?"

"Yeah, we're both fine. The windows got all shattered and there was some other damage, but luckily that was it. Nothing happened to us."

She shook her head, still in disbelief. "Fuck. I can't believe he… I mean, he gets into fights and does stupid shit all the time, but this is just… I don't know. I really don't know. What the hell's wrong with him? He needs to go to jail. You called the police, right?

"Yeah, but… I told'em I didn't know who did it."

"What? Why?"

"If I tell'em who did it, then I gotta tell my parents about everything else and… I don't think they're ready for that right now. And I don't think I'm ready for that either."

"So you're just gonna let him get away with this?"

"Well, right now, I don't know what else I can do."

When I first met Jasleen, she had this *thing* to her. And that *thing* was what I liked about her the most. It's hard to explain what it is, but in Punjabi the word for it is 'chaust'. That's what she was. It's a combination of aggressive and bold and sharp and a bunch of other words. It means a person has an edge to them. That they can't help but test every boundary in front of them. If there was a word to describe Jasleen, 'chaust' is what it would be.

But the next time I saw her, the night she told me she was pregnant, that part of her was gone. And whatever was left could never add up to who she was.

As I told her what happened at the restaurant, it was as if that missing part of her started coming back to life. At first, she was shocked and concerned, but as we continued talking, that shock and concern turned into anger. A fierce anger. And all of a sudden, she grabbed her purse and car keys and said, "Do you have anywhere to be right now?"

I said, "Why?"

"Let's go to my parents' house."

"For what?"

"I wanna tell them what happened. And I wanna see what they're gonna do about it."

"What can they really do?"

"I don't know, but if they could find a way to punish me for getting pregnant, then they can do something about him too."

I was taken aback. Hearing her talk like that almost made me forget about what happened. But I still didn't wanna go with her. I said, "Look, *you* can do that, but *I* don't wanna go there."

"Why not?"

"Cause it's gonna look like I came there to cry and complain about all of this."

"Who cares what it looks like? Look, this isn't some minor thing. It's a big deal."

"Yes, I know. I was there."

"So don't you think there should be some consequences for what he did?"

"Yeah, of course."

"Okay, so either you tell the police or you come with me. That's your two options." I just sat there, refusing to move, so she said, "Or lemme put it this way — either you come with me, or *I'm* gonna call the police and tell them who did it."

She was adamant, and I didn't have the energy to argue. So we took off to her parent's house, together.

She drove so fast I had to keep telling her to slow down. Each time I said it, she'd ease up on the gas pedal for a bit, but then, as if she couldn't help it, she'd speed back up. As we went up the hill, I started to get a little car sick and I wasn't even the one who was pregnant.

When we got there, Jasleen didn't bother knocking or ringing the bell. She used her key to open the door and walked right in. I had never seen her so determined. After looking around for a bit, we found the parents in the kitchen, along with Harman and Mahi, who were apparently in town. The dining table was set, and it looked like they were just getting ready to have lunch. They were all surprised to see us and immediately became worried. Jasleen's Mom, in Punjabi, said, "Jasleen? Is everything okay?"

Then her Dad said, "What's going on? What happened?"

Jasleen didn't waste any time getting to the point. "Have you talked to your nephew lately?"

He said, "What nephew?"

"Satti."

"No, why? What about him?"

"You don't know?"

"Know what? What are you talking about?"

"He came to Indo's restaurant last night. With a shotgun."

Everyone was taken aback. But Harman and his Dad's reactions were a little different than Mahi and the Mom.

Harman, with his eyes open wide, said, "What did he do?"

Jasleen looked over at me as if she wanted *me* to explain. I felt like a kid who got bullied at school and brought his Mom with him the next day to complain to the principal. I said, "Uhh... yeah, Satti was at the restaurant last night, making threats and stuff. And later on, after we closed... someone shot out our windows."

141

Jasleen's Mom walked over and asked, "Oh my god, are you okay?"

I said, "Yeah, I'm fine."

Mahi was shaken by the news. Harman and his Dad looked at each other but remained quiet. Jasleen noticed them and said, "Why aren't either of you saying anything?"

Her Dad, in Punjabi, said, "No, it's just… I don't know what to say. I can't believe he did that."

Something in his voice didn't sound right. Jasleen gave him a long stare and said, "Did you have something to do with this?"

Jasleen's Dad immediately became outraged. He yelled, "What does that mean? Why would I have something to do this?"

I was sure him raising his voice would make Jasleen back down, but she didn't. "I don't know… but there's something you're not telling me."

"There's nothing… I told you I'm just shocked about all of this."

"Then why don't you *sound* shocked?"

"What are you trying to say? Are you calling your own father a liar? Is that's what it's come to?"

"I'm not calling you anything, just answer the question!"

He turned to Jasleen's Mom and Mahi and said, "You see how she's talking to me?!"

But the two of them were looking at him just as suspiciously as Jasleen was. Jasleen's Mom said, "Just tell her you didn't do anything."

He said, "I don't have to tell her anything! Who does she think she is? First she disgraces us, then she comes in here accusing me of—"

Finally, Harman, who had been sitting there with his head in his hands, interrupted. "Dad!"

Everyone's attention turned to him.

"Stop. Just... stop." He took a deep breath. "We have to tell her."

His Dad's eyes widened, but he didn't respond. He seemed taken aback that Harman had raised his voice.

Harman turned to Jasleen. "Jasleen... you remember that night when the two of you came over for dinner?

Jasleen nodded.

"Well after you left, Thaiya [uncle] and Satti came by... and we told them what happened. At that point, we didn't know what to do... we were desperate, and it didn't seem like there was any solution to this whole thing. So Satti offered to help." He paused and took a deep breath. "And me and Dad... we agreed to let him."

Jasleen couldn't believe it. And neither could her Mom or Mahi. Or even me. Harman continued, "But there was one thing we made absolutely clear — that no matter what, he wasn't gonna start any trouble. And he promised us both he wouldn't. So that's why—"

Jasleen cut him off. "Wait, so you told the guy who got into a fight at *both* his sisters' weddings to not start any trouble? And then what? Just hoped for the best and looked the other way?"

Neither of them answered. Neither could even look her in the eyes.

Jasleen shook her head. "What is wrong with you guys? You know how he is, and you knew how he was gonna 'help', and you *still* let him do it?" Why, just so you could get your way? Is that all that matters to you?"

143

Suddenly, the anger in her voice was gone, and her eyes started to well up. She looked at her Dad with all the disappointment in the world and said, "Dad... when I found out I was pregnant... you know what the first thing I thought about was?" She paused. "It wasn't me or the baby... it was you. And how it was gonna make you feel. But what about you? When you found out I was pregnant... what was the first thing *you* thought about? Was it me? Was it about how hard my life was about to become? Was it about what you could do to make my life easier and what you could do to support me and help me? It wasn't, right? No... the first thing you thought about was yourself. Why is that? Why wasn't it the other way around? I thought *I* was the child, and *you* were the parent. I thought *I* was supposed to be selfish and stupid and immature, and *you* were supposed to look out for me. So why didn't you?"

He didn't have an answer. And Jasleen didn't wait for him to give her one. "All my life Dad, all I wanted was for you to accept me, but... I don't care anymore. It's not worth anything to me." Then she turned to me and said, "Let's go."

And we walked out of that house with no intention of ever coming back.

She finally let go. The shame, the guilt, the fear, the doubt... none of it was hers anymore. It was almost like she had gone home just to give it all back.

But it was a painful liberation. On the drive back, she tried to be stoic about it, but as soon as we walked into the apartment, she broke down. It was hard enough losing her father, but she never expected to lose her brother too. It seemed like an unfair price to pay for something that should have been hers to begin with.

In the end, it took something happening to *me* for Jasleen to finally stand up to her Dad. That really got to me. In the beginning, Jasleen was someone I was attracted to. Then I got to know her a little bit and she turned into someone I liked. When I found out she was pregnant and we started on this crazy journey together, she became someone I cared about and respected. By the end of that weekend, she was someone who would forever be a part of me.

Chapter 16 – A Knock at the Door

I decided to spend that night with Jasleen to make up for the night before, and we ended up sharing the same bed. Nothing happened between us. I guess so much happened during the day that neither of us was up for anything more.

When I woke up the next morning, I forgot where I was until I saw her sleeping next to me. It was kinda nice waking up next to her, and I just sat there for a while, watching her. Wondering if she was having good dreams or bad ones. Wondering if I was in them. Wondering where we'd go from there.

Her eyes opened. I looked away but wasn't fast enough. She said, "Were you watching me sleep?"

I said, "No."

She smiled. "How cute."

I rolled my eyes.

She yawned, then looked up at the ceiling and just stared at it for a while. Finally, she put her hand on her stomach and said, "I think it's gonna be a girl."

I looked down at her hand. "Is that what you want?"

She thought about it. "Yeah."

"How come?"

She shrugged. "I don't know. People always want boys. Girls they usually just kinda accept. And maybe that's what makes the difference... being wanted instead of accepted."

I nodded. "Maybe."

She turned to me and said, "What about you? What do *you* want?"

I said, "Me?"

The question caught me off guard. Who was *I* to want something? Before I could even think about how to answer, Jasleen's phone started vibrating and she reached over and grabbed it off the nightstand. It was Harman. She let it ring for a while, staring at his picture on her screen, then she looked over at me. I shrugged and said, "Answer."

She put it on speaker. "Hello."

He said, "Hey, uhh... were you sleeping?"

"No. What do you want?"

"Look... I'm..." He let out a heavy breath. "... I'm so, so sorry. If I thought he would go that far, I never would've let him get involved. You have to believe that."

"Okay."

"But still, I mean... it was wrong. It was very wrong. I was just, like I said, desperate. I had never seen Dad like that before, and I was worried something would happen to him, you know, like another heart attack or... something even worse. I'm not trying to make excuses... I just... I was just scared Jasleen, that's all it was."

Jasleen wasn't moved. Or at least she was acting like she wasn't. She said, "Yeah okay, sure. Was there anything else?"

He said, "Uhh, yeah actually, I wanna give Indo a call too, to apologize. Can you give me his number?"

"Well he's here right now, so you can talk to him. You're on speaker."

"Oh. Uhh, hey man."

I said, "What's up?"

"So, I mean, I wanna apologize to you too. From the bottom of my heart man, I'm so sorry. This was seriously the biggest mistake of my life."

"Yeah, it is what it is man. I don't know."

"And listen… I'm not justifying what he did, not at all. It doesn't make it any less bad, but I talked to Satti and he swears he thought no one was inside the restaurant. He wasn't trying to hurt anyone."

"Well, he showed up at the place with a shotgun, so I mean, what else was he trying to do?"

"Like I said bro, I'm not trying to justify it. And if you don't believe me, I don't blame you. But I know what he is and I know what he isn't… and he's not a killer. That much I'm sure about."

"If you say so."

"And also, if there's anything we can do to help out with your restaurant — we're willing to pay for the damages or do anything else we can."

"Nah, we're good. Thanks."

He sounded sincere I guess, but neither me or Jasleen was ready to forgive and forget.

Before he hung up, he asked to speak to Jasleen again, so I handed the phone back to her. She said, "Yeah?"

Harman said, "Hey I just wanted to ask — have you heard from Mahi?"

"No, why?"

"Oh… no nothing, I was just wondering. Alright, I'll talk to you later."

"Hold on, what's going on? What happened?"

Harman was quiet for a moment, then said, "Well, uhh…

actually... you weren't the only person that walked out of the house yesterday."

Me and Jasleen looked at each other, surprised. I could tell Mahi was upset when she found out what her husband had done, but she wasn't the type to just take off like that. Jasleen asked, "Where did she go?"

Harman said, "Well she was really quiet for a while after you guys left, then outta the blue she said she wanted to go to her parents' house. I tried to talk her out of it but she wouldn't listen. And now she's not answering my calls."

After the phone call, Jasleen felt responsible and I got a little worried about her. After everything she had been through, I didn't want her to slip back into the world of guilt. I said, "Yo, that has nothing to do with you. That's completely on your Dad and your brother. No one else."

She nodded and said, "Yeah, I know."

Normally, that conversation would've lasted an hour and a half, and I'd have a migraine by the end of it. I breathed a sigh of relief.

Jasleen had class that morning, so she took off early and I was left at the apartment by myself. All I could think about was Mahi leaving the house. Mahi was a lot of things, but she wasn't impulsive, so what would make her do something so drastic?

After taking a shower and eating a bowl of Lucky Charms, I got ready to go. But just as I was about to leave, there was a knock at the door. At first I thought it was Candice; she was supposed to be back in the afternoon. But then I realized that Candice wouldn't knock on her own door. I opened it. It was Mahi.

We both just stared at each other for a moment. Then I said,

"Hey… uhh… you here to see Jasleen?"

Mahi said, "No, I just talked to her."

"Oh."

"Can I come in?"

"Yeah."

I led her inside, and we sat down in the living room, across from each other.

She looked so much more put together now than she did when we were younger. It was like she had grown into herself.

I said, "What's up, what brings you over?"

She said, "Nothing, just… the restaurant… I wanted to tell you I'm really sorry."

I shrugged and said, "It's okay, I knew something like that could happen."

The restaurant was just as much a part of her childhood as it was mine. We used to be there all the time — stealing freshly-made ladoos from the kitchen, getting in trouble for running around in the dining area, putting together the pink folding boxes we sold sweets in. It was like a second home to both of us when we were kids.

"Are your parents okay?"

"Yeah, they're just glad it wasn't worse." There was brief silence, then I said, "So… where you coming from?"

She said, "From my parents' house," and didn't explain any further.

There was another silence. Neither one of us knew where to take the conversation, and she started fidgeting with the hair tie on her wrist. Finally, she said, "It's so crazy. Such a small world."

I said "Yeah… too small."

"You know what's funny? When Harman first met 'Jasleen's new boyfriend', he said he was a jerk."

I let out a laugh.

"But I told him that maybe this guy was just mad about getting attacked by Dad, and all we had to do was sit him down and talk to him nicely… and then he'd understand." She shook her head. "If only I knew who we were dealing with."

I smiled.

She said, "I always told you you should've been a lawyer."

"Yeah, I don't know about all that."

Mahi smiled. She looked around for a moment, then turned back to me and asked, "So, how did you and Jasleen meet?"

"At a club."

"Oh yeah, I remember her telling me that." She paused for a moment, then got this funny look on her face and said, "You know, I've never been to a club."

It was kind of surprising but made sense. She was never really the partying type and got married right after graduating. I said, "Well yeah, I mean, only cool people are allowed in clubs… so how would you have even gotten in?"

She laughed. Back in the day, she would have had some sort of clever comeback, but that day, I guess she was just happy to be insulted after so long. She said, "So, are you excited about becoming a father?"

"I don't know what I am. Everything happened so quick."

She raised her eyebrows. "It happened quick?"

"Yeah."

"Jasleen didn't mention that part."

Then she smiled and I finally realized what she meant. I laughed. Hard. That was the closest thing to a dirty joke I had ever heard her tell. I said, "Damn, woman… what has marriage done to you? Does your Mom know you talk like that?"

She said, "No, why? Are you gonna tell on me?"

We were talking like we were teenagers again. As if everything that had gone wrong since then, had never gone wrong. For a moment, it was like we went somewhere else.

Then her phone started to ring and we came back to where we started. She didn't answer it, but after she checked who was calling, she said, "I should get going." I'm guessing it was Harman.

She got up and started heading towards the door. Just as she was walking out, I said, "Hey." She stopped and looked back at me. I said, "You remember how I didn't come to your wedding cause I was sick?"

She said, "Yeah."

"I was faking it."

She froze up. Then, she asked, "How come?"

I thought about it for a bit, and said, "It's probably better I don't say anything else."

She was disappointed. She looked down at the ground and became lost in her thoughts for a little while. Finally, she looked up and said, "You know… that day when they told me you were sick, and that you weren't coming… I was hoping you were faking it."

Now *I* was the one who couldn't move. I said, "Why?"

She took a breath and said, "I probably shouldn't say anything else either." And she left.

Chapter 17 – Reunited

Living a lie is a full-time commitment. You don't get a break from it. Not even when you're sleeping. It's something that involves every part of your being, every second of every day, and after a while, you don't even know who you are or where you are. You're a person that doesn't really exist, in a place that doesn't really exist. And you can only live like that for so long. *My* time was up.

If me and Jasleen were gonna be together, there couldn't be any secrets between us. So I decided I was gonna tell her the truth about Mahi. The whole truth. How we grew up together, how I felt about her, and how I let her get away. I didn't know how Jasleen would take it, but if a relationship was what we were building... I knew it couldn't be built on a lie.

That night, I had the weirdest dream. With most dreams, I know I'm dreaming, but this was one of those where I could swear it was real. I was at a family party at one of my cousins' houses in Vallejo. I don't know what we were celebrating, but I could tell it was something big because of who was there. Whenever you see *very* distant relatives at an event, you know it's important, and I remember seeing Harry, my Mom's sister's husband's brother's brother-in-law, walking around with a drink in his hand.

At a certain point, everyone gathered in the family room and they brought out a giant, colorful cake and set it down on the coffee table. I still didn't know who or what it was for. All of the kids excitedly knelt down in front of it, and the light from the candles made their faces glow. Finally, a little boy and his mom walked through the crowd, they stepped around the kids, and sat down behind the cake. I had never seen the boy before but I recognized the mom. Raveena.

She had gained some weight and kinda looked like an auntie. I could tell she was the same person, but it felt like we were in different lifetimes. Like she had already moved on to the next one. Right away, I got that strange feeling you get when you haven't seen someone in a while and there's tension between the two of you. I started looking for someone to hide behind, but before I could find anyone big enough, she spotted me in the crowd.

At first she was surprised to see me, but then she smiled and gave me a head nod. I was a little taken aback. After I nodded back, she gestured at me to join them. I tried to politely turn her down, but she kept insisting, so finally I made my way over. When I reached her, she looked down at her son and said, "This is your Indo mamma [uncle], say 'Hi'."

The kid, who was probably 5 or 6, looked up at me and said, "Hi Indo mamma."

I said "Hello" and looked up at Raveena. "He looks just like you."

"Really? People usually say that about his sister but never about this little brat." She paused and looked at me, then gave me a warm smile. "Look at you. You're all grown up now."

"Yeah… I don't know how it happened."

She laughed, and we spent the next few minutes catching up. She told me about everything — her kids, her husband, her job, her house — but she never once mentioned what happened between me and her Dad. In all the years since then, whenever Raveena came to my mind, that was the first thing I thought about. And I always figured that when I saw her again, *if* I saw her again, that would be the first thing we'd talk about. Like it was something we had to address and figure out before we could move on. But it seemed like Raveena had moved on a long time ago. It didn't even seem like it mattered to her anymore. She had gone on into the future, and I was still in the past.

When I woke up the next morning, I didn't know what to make of that dream. I laid in bed for the longest time, trying to figure it out, but I couldn't. Eventually, I decided that maybe it was just a dream. Maybe they're *all* just dreams.

While I was getting ready, I tried to imagine how Jasleen would react to what I was about to tell her. How she'd look, how she'd feel, what she'd say. I thought about all the questions she would ask me, and all the answers I would give her. But more than anything, I wondered if she'd forgive me for keeping it a secret… and what would happen if she didn't.

When I got to Candice's apartment and approached the door, I noticed a pair of shoes on the ground. Men's dress shoes. The door was slightly open so I walked inside without knocking and saw Jasleen sitting on the couch in the living room. Sitting across from her, was her Dad.

Right away, I knew something strange was going on because he didn't look at me the way he normally did. There was humility in his eyes. And that humility scared me a thousand times more than the fury I was used to seeing. I said, "Sat Sri

Akal" and he said it back.

Then he said, "It's good that you came because I wanted to talk to you too." I hesitantly sat down on a chair away from the two of them, and he continued, "How are you? How are your parents?"

I said, "We're okay."

He nodded, then leaned slightly forward in his chair, and continued in Punjabi. "Look… I'm sorry for what happened to your restaurant. I know it's not just a restaurant to you and your family — it's something a lot more. And seeing this happen to it… it must have been hard. And I take responsibility for causing all of you that pain."

As much as I wanted to, I couldn't doubt his sincerity. He went on, "But whether you believe me or not, that's not the type of people we are. We never *have* been. This was just a mistake… a big mistake." He paused again. "I'm not gonna ask you both to forgive me, because maybe I don't deserve it. I just came here to tell you… that I give up. This whole thing has gone too far… and it needs to end."

Then he said something I wouldn't have expected him to say in a million years. "Whatever you guys want to do, whenever you want to get married, I'm okay with it. I just want my family back, because my family means more to me than anything." He started to tear up.

The whole time he was talking, Jasleen was trying to seem indifferent, but the sight of her Dad crying was too much for her to bear. As hard as she tried, she couldn't stop herself from becoming emotional. Then her Dad, still in tears, stood up and said, "You guys think about it. I'll get going." But Jasleen stopped him. She stood up, walked over and buried her face in his chest. He put his arms around her, and before I even knew what happened… father and daughter were reunited.

He did what people rarely do. And what Punjabi fathers *never* do. Change.

When most people get hurt, they get angry. I guess it's a way to hide their vulnerability. But it's hard to sympathize with somebody who's angry. Anger just brings about more anger. When Jasleen found out what her Dad had done, she was hurt, and that's all she showed him. There was no cover-up. And when you can see the pain you caused someone, you have no choice but to look at yourself and what you've done. You can fight against anger, but you can't fight against pain, and seeing it in its purest form has a profound effect on a person. And that's what I think happened to Jasleen's Dad.

The war was over, and me and Jasleen won. And it was the worst thing that could have ever happened.

Chapter 18 – Say the Word

You think you know what you want until you get it. I liked my life a lot better with Jasleen in it… but the idea of actually getting married had never even crossed my mind. I guess I just didn't think it would get to that point. When I gave Jasleen's parents my terms, I didn't consider that they might accept them. But they did. And now there were no more objections left for me to make.

Over the next few days, I got three phone calls and each one felt like another nail in my coffin. The first one was from a random number, while I was washing my car. I picked up and a subdued voice on the other side said, "What's up bro?"

I said, "What's up… who's this?"

"Satti."

My last interaction with him involved bullets flying through my windows so I immediately got the urge to reach through the phone and choke the life out of that fucker. But Satti wasn't looking for a fight. He said, "Hey look man, before you hang up, I just wanna say… I'm really sorry about what happened. I didn't mean for it to get that far. I was just looking out for my cousin, you know, and it got outta hand. But still, it shouldn't have. It's just that… when your boy busted out that gun, I took it as a threat to me and my family… so I had to defend myself."

He kept going back and forth between apologizing and trying to justify what he did. He went on. "But I swear bro, all we were trying to do was scare you. Nothing else. I've gotten into some crazy shit before, but there's a line I would never cross. I mean, unless I had no choice. But the most important thing you need to know is — when we shot out the windows, for sure it was wrong and we shouldn't have done it... but we had no idea anyone was inside. We thought y'all had left already. And when I found out you and your pops were still there... fuck man, I felt so bad. I've never regretted anything so much in my life. I haven't even slept right since then, I'm telling you. So yeah, I wish it never happened, but I can't take it back now... so I hope you believe me and, you know, accept my apology and stuff."

As exhausting as his 'apology' was to listen to, I believed him when he said he thought the restaurant was empty. And as much as I wanted him to pay for what he did, I didn't have it in me to go after any kinda revenge. After taking a moment, I said, "Uhh, yeah... I'm not gonna say it's all good man, cause it ain't. But, whatever, it's over... gotta move on."

He said, "Thanks for understanding bro. You're right, we gotta put this behind us. We're bout to be family."

The next phone call came from Jasleen's Mom. She wanted to check in on me to see how I was doing, but her main reason for calling was to invite me to their grand 30th anniversary party, which was now just a few days away. This was a huge gesture because everyone in their entire world would be there. I figured they'd wanna keep me hidden until me and Jasleen got married, but apparently I was ready to be revealed. She also wanted me to arrange a meeting between my parents and them as soon as possible. I had managed to keep them out of all this as long as I could, but now it was only a matter of time before the secret had to be let out. I told her I'd talk to them and get back to her.

With me being caught up in the aftermath of the restaurant incident, and Jasleen busy with preparations for the party, we didn't have time to see each other for a while. After playing phone tag for a few days, we were finally able to connect one night just before I went to bed. As soon as the conversation began, I heard something in her voice I hadn't heard in forever — happiness. And why wouldn't there be? All was right in the kingdom again. She was back home, Mahi and Harman had made up, and her parents had accepted her unconditionally. But she wasn't calling to tell me all that. She had a very important question to ask me. "Hey, so, we were all wondering... since you're gonna be at the party, right?"

"Yeah."

"Umm... what are we gonna call you? Like, when we introduce you to people?"

"Indo."

She laughed. "No, fool. Like who are you... to us?"

"Are you gonna make some announcement or something?"

"No, no, nothing like that. But you know, people might ask who you are? So what do we say?"

"Yeah, I don't know."

She was quiet for a few seconds. "Okay, so... my Mom was thinking... maybe... we can call you... my fiancé."

I started coughing.

"Woah, you okay?"

"Yeah, yeah, I'm good. Uhh... fiancé?"

"Yeah, I mean it wouldn't be anything *official*. But we have to call you *something* right?"

What could I really say? After everything they had given in on, it wasn't an unreasonable request. So I agreed to it.

It was all becoming too real. As scary as shotgun blasts through our restaurant windows were, they were less scary than this. I was nowhere near ready to get married, but that's exactly where this train was headed. And there was no getting off.

Towards the end of the week, we were finally able to get someone to come by the restaurant and repair the windows. While I was there supervising, Lucky's car pulled into the parking lot. Just what I needed — an 'I told you so,' followed by a call for revenge.

As he walked in and assessed the damage, his eyes got wide. I was behind the bar, watching him, and I had never seen him so overwhelmed. He came over and said, "Fuck bro... I'm sorry."

I said, "Yeah man. It was pretty crazy."

He said, "No, I mean... *I'm* sorry. This shit was because of me, wasn't it?"

"What are you talking about?

"The gun. That's why they took it this far."

"Nah bruh... he just needed an excuse. If it wasn't that, it would've been something else."

Lucky wasn't so sure. He sat down on one of the stools and said, "So why'd you act like you didn't know who did it?"

I said, "You know why."

He nodded, then took another look at the windows. "So where's *that* whole situation stand now?"

I sighed. "You want a drink?"

He acted like he didn't hear me. "Come again? *You're* asking *me* if I want a drink? On a Thursday? At 4pm?"

I didn't answer.

"Fuck bro, is it that bad?"

"You want one or not?"

"Are *you* drinking?"

"Yeah."

"Okay, well, I can't let you drink alone."

I grabbed a bottle of Crown, led him to one of the corner booths and poured a couple drinks. And as we sat there having one after another, I explained the situation and opened up to Lucky about how I was feeling. Feelings weren't exactly something we ever shared with each other, so it really caught him off guard.

Lucky had a much more simple way of looking at life than I did, and sometimes complicated problems require simple solutions. After taking everything in, he said, "Well... the way I see it, there's really only two things you can do."

I waited for him to elaborate.

He said, "What does this girl think of you?"

"What do you mean?"

"I mean, you did all this for her, so she must be grateful, right?"

"I guess so."

"You *guess* so?"

"Okay, I mean, yeah, I'm sure she is. Why?"

"Well, then maybe you should just tell her the truth. Tell her you want out. Maybe she'll understand."

"Even if she did understand, where would that leave *her*?"

"That's for her to figure out. You helped her get *this* far. She can take it the rest of the way."

"Look bro, that sounds all well and good, but I made a commitment to her. And she didn't ask me to do that, I chose to. So if I back out on that now — what's my word really worth?"

Lucky accepted my reasoning.

I said, "So what's the other thing?"

He said, "Uhh… I don't know if you really wanna know."

I waited for him to tell me anyway.

He poured another drink for each of us, then said, "Who's the real father of the baby?"

I told him what I knew. "Some dude named Prince. I think he lives in Fremont."

"And he has no idea Jasleen's pregnant?"

I shook my head.

Lucky said, "Well… what if he found out?

"How would he find out?"

Lucky shrugged. "Don't worry about that part."

Lucky was the kind of guy who was connected to everybody. He was like the Punjabi Kevin Bacon. There were six degrees of separation between him and every Punjabi person in North America. So, I didn't doubt he could make it happen. But I still didn't understand why he would want to. "What are you trying to say?"

He said, "I think you know."

At that point, we were about halfway through the bottle, so it took me a minute to figure it out. But once I did, I was more than a little disturbed by it. I said, "Nah man, that would be fucked up."

He said, "Is it more fucked up than passing off someone else's kid as your own?"

"Dude, you don't understand. From everything I've heard, this guy is the biggest piece of shit in the world. That's the whole reason she didn't tell him in the first place."

"That doesn't matter bro. This is *his* kid. I mean, put yourself in his shoes — if you had a kid out there somewhere, wouldn't you wanna know about it? Wouldn't you think you deserved to?"

The more he talked, the more sense he made. And the more sense he made, the more thought I gave to what he was saying. But eventually, I came to the same conclusion. "Look, I get what you're saying... but I can't do that to her."

He said, "Well then what are you gonna do? You gonna sacrifice your whole life for this chick? Just go on and on forever, living a lie? Look, you felt bad for her, you played captain save-a-hoe, and that's all good, but at a certain point, you gotta think about yourself. And what if you go ahead and marry her, and *then* this fool finds out? What then? Don't you think that's gonna be a lot worse? Because the truth always comes out bro... there's a reason they say that shit. And it's a lot better that it comes out *now* than later, *especially* for her. So all you have to do is say the word... and I promise you I'll get you out of this mess."

Lucky waited for me to respond, but we still had half a bottle left to go. And if I was gonna give him an answer, I didn't wanna be sober enough to remember what it was.

Chapter 19 – The Anniversary Party

Jasleen's parents, like my parents, and a lot of other immigrant parents, came to this country with very little. They got married young and had kids young, and after that, their lives weren't about dreams or aspirations — they were about survival. Survival in a foreign land with a foreign culture and a foreign language. And they dealt with all of that just so their kids could be American. They didn't complain or ask for any reward or recognition... they just did what they had to do. And they did it happily.

This anniversary party was Harman and Jasleen's way of honoring their parents for everything they had done. And they wanted to make it a night their parents would never forget. The party was being held at the fanciest banquet hall in the Bay Area, being catered by a Michelin-starred Punjabi restaurant, and they were flying in a world-renowned DJ from the UK. Every single one of their relatives, friends, and acquaintances was invited, and now, I was invited too.

On the night of the party, they asked me to come to the house, because they were hoping we could all leave for the hall together. I figured I would just show up by myself and blend into the crowd, but apparently they wanted to make me a prominent guest.

The drive up the hill was quiet this time. An eerie kind of quiet. The weather was calm, the sky was clear, and the world felt settled, in a very unsettling kind of way. Even the voice in my head that would normally be talking to me, had nothing left to say.

When I got there, Harman answered the door and I immediately noticed a different energy, not just from him but from the entire house. The last three times I was there, it was like going into enemy territory and I went in prepared for war. But now all of a sudden, there was peace. And it was unnerving. I didn't know what to do with peace... I was much more comfortable with war.

Harman said, "Hey Indo. Good to see you again. Come on in." He had never called me by my name before. It was strange.

He walked me to the living room, where his Dad was sitting on the sofa. The Dad got up and said, "Kiddha Inderjit." Even stranger hearing *him* say my name. He greeted me with a warm but wary smile. First time I had ever seen him smile. There was water, club soda, a fancy ice bucket, a bottle of Crown, and some old-fashioned glasses on the table. Father and son were pre-gaming.

He told Harman to pour a drink for me and I said "No, I'm good."

Then in Punjabi, he said, "This will make you more good."

Since it was a new beginning, I said, "Okay" and the next thing I knew, I was sitting there, drinking with the two of them. It was about as strange a situation as you could imagine. I still couldn't believe they were trying to accept me. All my years of living in a Punjabi world told me this wasn't supposed to be happening... but it was. I wanted to think it was some kind of trap… but it wasn't.

The mood was awkward and we all felt it, but after a while the alcohol started to kick in and we began to loosen up a little. Jasleen's Dad looked at me and in Punjabi, said, "You know this is the first time Harman's drinking with me."

I said, "Really?"

"Yeah, he's not really a big drinker. He's a good boy."

I nodded.

He said, "What about you?"

I said, "Uhh… yeah, I'm not such a good boy."

He smiled and said, "That's okay… I'm not either." We all laughed.

One drink turned into two, which turned into three, and before I knew it, I was feeling tipsy. At that point, for whatever reason, I decided I wanted to give myself a tour of the house. I got up, with my drink in hand, and started heading towards the hallway. Harman stopped me. "Where you going?"

"Uhh… the bathroom."

"Oh, okay. You know where it's at right?"

"Yeah, I think I remember."

"Hey, while you're at it, can you ask the ladies how much longer they're gonna be?"

"Yeah, sure."

I continued on and went down the hall until I reached the family room. On one of the walls was a giant collage of pictures. Pictures of Harman and Jasleen as little kids. Pictures of the parents from trips they went on. Pictures from birthdays, holidays, and parties. I went through'em all, one by one, learning the story of their family. And then I got to the part of the story that never should have happened. I got to the pictures of Harman and Mahi's wedding.

Before that moment, I hadn't seen any images from that day. Didn't want to. But now they were all staring me in the face. Mahi as a bride, Harman as a groom, the rituals, the moments, the happiness and the joy. It was like someone wanted to remind me that that day really happened. And that I *let* it happen.

On the other side of the family room was a long, windy staircase. I walked over and started carefully climbing up, as the buzz from the whiskey got stronger. For some reason, all the lights were out, and the only thing I had to guide me was this long, fancy chandelier hanging from the ceiling, in between the staircase. Once I made it up, I took another sip of my drink, walked through the loft, and down another hallway until I reached a half-open door. I peeked inside.

Mahi was sitting on a bed. She was putting on a necklace, and was all decked out, wearing this long, rose gold colored suit. I was mesmerized. And as I stared at her, I noticed the resemblance between the shape of her and the shape of the hole in my soul.

I gently pushed open the door. She turned her head and the sight of me startled her. I said, "Hey" as I walked inside.

She said, "Hey... what's going on?"

"Umm, your husband... he was asking how much longer you guys are gonna be."

"Oh, yeah, we should be down pretty soon."

"Cool, cool. Where's Jasleen?"

"She's just helping her Mom get ready."

I nodded and started looking around at the room. After nervously watching me for a bit, she said, "You look nice."

168

I said, "Thanks... you don't look too bad yourself."

She smiled.

We were both silent for a moment, then she said, "So... I guess we're gonna be family now."

I nodded. "Yeah... just not in the way we thought."

"Huh?" She acted like she didn't hear me, but I knew she did.

I shook my head and said, "Nothing."

I started to turn around, but then I stopped. I looked at Mahi and said, "Hey, you know uhh... I kinda lied to you about something."

She became a little concerned. "What?"

"You remember when I came here for that dinner? And I told you... I didn't know Jasleen was your sister-in-law?"

She nodded.

"Well, that wasn't completely true. Actually, it wasn't true at all. I knew... the whole time. And I think... that was the reason I got involved in all of this."

I expected her to be shocked, but she looked scared. Then I noticed that her eyes weren't looking at me... they were looking over my shoulder. Suddenly, I got this sick feeling in my stomach that something had gone terribly wrong. I turned around and saw Jasleen in the doorway.

She was standing there like a statue. I didn't know how much she heard, but judging by the devastation in her eyes, I knew it was more than enough.

Before anyone could do or say anything, Jasleen's Mom came walking down the hallway, saying, "It's getting late, you guys need to get going." When she reached the doorway and saw me standing in the room, she smiled and said, "Sat Sri Akal, Inderjit."

I barely got out the words but managed to say "Sat Sri Akal" back.

She said, "Okay, now hurry up and go."

We all just stood there, unable to move.

She looked at all of us, confused, and said, "What are you waiting for?" Finally, Jasleen walked away.

Before I knew it, we were on our way to the hall. Jasleen was driving, I was in the passenger seat, and Mahi and Harman were in the back. The plan was for us to head to the hall early, and the parents to come later and make their big entrance. Between me, Jasleen, and Mahi, there was the most suffocating tension, but Harman didn't pick up on it at all... because he was drunk out of his mind. I guess he really wasn't a drinker, because that little bit of whiskey turned him into a completely different person. He wouldn't stop talking the entire way there, even though the rest of us barely said a word.

When we pulled into the parking lot, there were already some guests there, so as soon as we got out of the car, the meeting and greeting began. Drunk Harman started loudly and proudly introducing me to anyone he could find. "Hey this is my future brother-in-law!" as if we were the best of friends. Mahi tried to get him to tone it down, but he had no interest in doing that.

Meanwhile, Jasleen was putting on the happiest face she could put on. "Oh my god Massi [auntie], you look so pretty." "Did you lose weight Massar [uncle]? Is Massi not feeding you?" Despite everything going on, she somehow found it in her to still be her charming self. But every once in a while, I'd catch her looking over at me like she was desperate for an explanation. And I'd look back at her, desperate to give her one.

After greeting a bunch of strangers, we finally ran into some people I recognized: The Aunt and the Uncle, Satti's parents. There was some question about whether or not they were even gonna come to party, because they were upset with Jasleen's Dad about giving in to me and Jasleen. But apparently, they decided to. We said "Sat Sri Akal" to them, and they said it back without any enthusiasm and quickly walked away.

"Look at these cute couples!" I turned around and saw Candice walking towards us. She was wearing this super fancy maroon sari with a silver necklace, giant earrings, bangles, and a tikka on her forehead. As soon as Harman saw her, he said, "Damn girl, look at you!"

She laughed. "Are you okay?"

"I'm better than okay."

"Yeah, I can tell."

Candice hugged both Mahi and Jasleen and they all spent a few moments talking about each other's outfits, the way girls do. Then Candice turned to me and smiled. "Well, well. Look who got himself invited to the party."

I let out a laugh.

She said, "You are something else my friend."

I said, "I try to be."

Then she nodded at Jasleen. "See, I told you — make sure to hang on to this one. Aren't you glad you listened to me?"

Jasleen did her best to smile.

Candice looked at all of us and said, "Let's take a picture!"

She pulled out her phone, extended her hand to take a selfie

171

and we all gathered behind her. Harman put both of his arms around Mahi, while me and Jasleen awkwardly stood next to each other. Candice looked at the frame on her phone, then turned back to us. "Okay, can you two take a lesson from the married people please?"

Harman and Mahi looked towards us and Harman said, "Seriously guys... you'd think it'd be the other way around."

Candice said, "I know, right?"

Mahi saw the uneasy looks on our faces and said, "It's okay — they're just worried about all the people around."

Harman said, "You think this guy really cares about what people think?"

Me and Jasleen looked at each other, and silently decided to go along with what they wanted. I put my arm around Jasleen, and Candice said, "There you go, thank you." We all smiled, and she took the picture.

As we stepped into the hall, we were all overwhelmed by how it looked. The building itself was from the 1800s, so it had that classical architecture, but it was decorated like a modern, glamorous ball. There was gold and violet light covering every inch of the walls, crystal chandeliers hanging from the ridiculously high ceilings, elaborate bouquet centerpieces on each of the tables, and fancy candles scattered throughout that made the entire room glow. Punjabi parties are generally pretty extravagant, but this one felt like something out of a fairy tale.

Once we were inside, we were almost immediately separated. The girls set themselves up by the entrance with the Aunt and Uncle to greet everyone coming in, and me and Harman went around checking on the different areas of the hall — the

DJ booth, the bar, the kitchen, the stage — to make sure everything was in order. As we were doing that, the guests started pouring in, wave after wave, and I could feel the space filling up around me. I kept an eye on Jasleen, trying to find an opportunity to go over and talk to her, but the busier the party got, the harder it became to find one. Pretty soon, the room was completely packed and the party was in full swing.

Harman dragged me around, having me shake one hand after another, until we got to a hand I didn't want to shake... Satti's. He was standing by the bar with a couple other guys, and as soon as he saw me, he put on that famous fake smile of his and said, "Hey what's up bro?"

Even though we squashed things over the phone, the sight of him still made my fists clench up. I said, "What's up," in a dead serious tone and right away everyone could feel the tension between us. But Harman wasn't about to let us go down that road. Before anyone could say another word, he said, "Let's take shots!"

As Harman gave the order to the bartender, I turned back and started looking around for Jasleen. But I couldn't find her *or* Mahi. Somewhere along the way I lost track of them.

"Indo! Your drink." I turned back and Harman handed it to me. We all looked at each other, awkwardly, then touched glasses as Harman yelled, "Cheers fellas!"

I downed the shot and scanned the room again. Still didn't see them. I decided I was gonna go searching for them. I waited for Harman and the others to get lost in conversation and managed to slip away.

I walked through the tables, checked the buffet area, the lobby... no sign of them anywhere. Eventually, I started heading back to the bar, but on my way there I heard a voice behind me say, "What the fuck are *you* doing here?" I turned around. It was Paul, Mahi's brother.

I don't know why it never crossed my mind that Mahi's family would be at this party too. Of course they would. Seeing Paul was a trip, but I snapped myself out of it as quickly as I could and said, "Holy shit bro." He had a plate full of food in one hand and a drink in the other, and judging by the smile on his face it wasn't his first drink of the night. I gave him a hug.

He said, "Man, it's been a minute."

I said, "It's been a *few* minutes. How you been?"

"Been great — just livin' the family man life, you know."

"Oh yeah, you got a kid now, right?"

"Yup, a boy. Looks just like me."

I let out a laugh.

"Yeah, he's running around here somewhere. The wife's here too, you should come by our table and say hi."

"Yeah I'll do that for sure. But hey uhh, lemme catch up with you in a bit, I gotta—"

He cut me off. "Wait, what are you doing here again? Did Mahi invite you?"

"Huh? Oh, no... I'm uhh... I'm just a... friend of their daughter, Jasleen."

"Oh I see. I thought maybe you and Mahi were still talking or whatever."

"Yeah, not really. But like I said man, I'll see—"

He cut me off again. "You know bro, I've never said this to you before, but to tell you the truth — I always thought you two were gonna end up together. Just the way you guys were when you were kids... it was just... I don't know. Anyway bro, I'll let you go. I gotta get back to the family too."

The whole time we were talking, I was trying to end the conversation, but now for some reason, I wasn't in a hurry anymore. Paul took off.

Just as I was about to start scanning the room again, Mahi suddenly appeared in front of me. I said, "Hey, I just saw your brother."

She didn't respond. Instead, she quickly pulled me to a corner so we could talk in private. Then she looked around to make sure no one was listening and said, "The baby's not yours?"

I was shocked. "She told you?"

Mahi nodded. "Yeah."

I took a second to process what I had just heard, then said, "What else did she say?"

Just as she was about to answer, we heard, "Hey everybody! Thanks so much for being here tonight!

We both turned to the stage and saw MC Harman standing there, with a mic in his hand. Apparently, the alcohol still hadn't worn off. He started to give this incoherent but heartfelt speech about his parents. As he was talking, I turned back to Mahi so she could continue. She said, "She told me everything."

I said, "Hey, listen, as far as what I said earlier—"

She cut me off. "Look, you can explain that to me later. Right now, you really need to talk to Jasleen. She was *already* feeling sick all day, and now she's… *really* not doing good. And I'm starting to get worried about her."

"Where is she?"

Mahi pointed to a table on the other side of the room. Jasleen was standing next to it, talking to some relatives. She still had that smile on her face that was so easy to see through.

Harman wrapped up his speech and said, "My parents are about to make their grand entrance, so please everyone, find your way back to your seats." Mahi gave me one last look and walked back to her table. I looked around and saw that everybody in the hall was starting to sit down — except for the men at the bar, who never follow directions. I headed towards them as Harman gave the microphone back to the DJ.

As I ordered another drink, the DJ made the big introduction. "Ladies and gentlemen, please welcome Mr. and Mrs. Gill!"

The DJ put on a romantic Bollywood song, the parents walked in and everyone stood up and applauded. They slowly passed through the crowd, waving to people and soaking in the love. Once they got to the stage, the DJ got back on the mic. "Ladies and gentleman, another big round of applause for the lovely couple!" There was another extended ovation, until they brought out the cake, and Harman, Mahi and Jasleen joined them on stage.

It was at that point that Harman started looking around the hall. At first, I didn't think anything of it, but then it hit me — he was looking for *me*. Fuck. I tried to blend into the crowd, hoping he wouldn't find me. Then Harman asked the DJ for the microphone and said, "Hey, you know what? We're here to celebrate my parents' anniversary... but that's not all we have to celebrate tonight. As some of you have already found out, we have a new member of the family... our little Jasleen just got engaged and her fiancé is here with us tonight."

The parents, Jasleen and Mahi all looked at him like, "What the hell are you doing?" This wasn't part of the script. Harman had gone rogue.

Eventually, I had no choice but to step forward. Harman saw me and said, "There he is! Come on stage bro. Don't be shy." And now, all of the hundreds of people in the hall had their eyes on *me*. It was the most terrifying thing I had ever experienced. In that moment, the magnitude of everything hit me, and I felt like a little kid who just wanted to run away. As I made my way to the stage, I thought about my parents who were sitting at home, probably watching TV, with absolutely no idea what their son was up to. What the fuck was I doing? How did I end up there?

And then I reached the stage and saw the answer to all my questions, standing there, wearing a rose-gold colored suit.

The DJ got back on the mic and said, "Now it's time for the first dance." Me, Jasleen, Mahi and Harman all backed off to make room for the parents. The lights changed color and the fog machine filled the dance floor with thick white clouds. As soon as the song began to play, everyone in the room became captivated. It was obvious both parents felt awkward as hell, but that only added to the charm of the whole thing. It was a magical moment, and we all got lost in it.

I looked over at Jasleen every once in a while, but she wouldn't make eye contact. Since we met, she had been so many things — afraid, angry, depressed, distraught — but this was something there wasn't even a word for. It was like I made up a brand new way to hurt someone.

As the song wound down, the DJ said, "Now I'd like to call all of the other couples here tonight to join Mr. and Mrs. Gill on the dance floor." This was my chance. I walked over to Jasleen and put my hand out. She looked at me, surprised, and for a moment I thought she was gonna turn me down. But finally, she put her hand in mine and let me lead her onto the dance floor.

We got into slow dance position and started making subtle movements to the music. What struck me right away was how pale she looked, so before I even got into my explanation, I asked, "Are you okay?"

She said, "No."

I didn't know how to respond.

Then she said, "I don't feel right."

I said, "Do you wanna go outside? Get some air?"

She shook her head.

We continued dancing, while I thought about where to begin. Finally, I said, "How come you told Mahi the baby's not mine?"

As soon as the words came out of my mouth, I regretted saying them. It wasn't so much what I was asking her, it was the fact that I said Mahi's name with such familiarity. Hearing that made her go even deeper into the hole she was in. She stared at me for a moment, then said, "Because it isn't."

It was at that point that some nervous teenager came up to Harman, who was dancing with Mahi, and whispered something into his ear. Me and Jasleen watched him, curiously. Judging by the look on Harman's face, it wasn't good news, so we drifted over to find out what was up. A suddenly sober Harman told us there was some sorta argument going on in the lobby, involving Satti. He said, "I'm gonna go check it out."

Mahi got worried and said, "I'll come with you."

"No, you guys stay here and act normal. I don't want people to get alarmed. It might not even be a big deal."

"Okay, but don't go by yourself."

That was the cue for me to volunteer. I said, "I'll go."

He said, "No bro. This isn't your problem."

"Well, according to you I'm the 'new member of the family,' so it kinda is."

We headed over, trying to draw as little attention to us as possible. Harman was pissed off. Every Punjabi family has that one guy you have to worry about at a party. A guy who's always looking for a fight. And if he doesn't find one, one usually ends up finding *him*. Harman said, "I can't believe this guy. I even had a talk with him today and told him not to start any shit."

When we reached the lobby, there was a standoff between two groups. On one side was Satti and his boys; on the other was a group of guys wearing regular street clothes. Satti seemed like the type who had a lot of enemies, so I figured this group was just one of the many, but as soon as Harman saw their leader, he said, "What the hell is *he* doing here?"

I said, "Who?"

He said, "Prince."

It took a few seconds for that name to ring a bell, but when it finally rang, the sound was deafening. Of all the times and all the places Jasleen's ex-boyfriend could have picked to confront her... he had to pick *this* time, and *this* place. What had I done?

As soon as I saw him, I knew exactly why Jasleen decided to hide everything from him. There was a fury in his eyes that was beyond any logic or understanding. He was possessed. And what really made the sight of him disturbing was that he was so put together and good-looking. If you saw him walking down the street, you'd never think he was capable of becoming a monster. When Jasleen described the love/hate, back and forth nature of their relationship, I could never really wrap my head around it. But now that I could put a face to it, I understood it completely.

Harman immediately threw himself in between the two groups and tried to reason with Prince. He said, "Look man, you gotta get outta here. This is a party for my parents... I don't want any trouble."

But Prince, who looked like he'd been drinking, refused to leave. "I need to talk to Jassi."

"I'm sorry man. That's not gonna happen. She's moved on — you just gotta accept that and move on too."

"I'm not leaving here 'til I talk to her."

Then Satti jumped in. "Yo you either leave on your own or we're gonna *make* your bitch ass leave."

Any amount of progress Harman would make, Satti would ruin with threats and insults. As the conflict escalated, the crowd around us got bigger and bigger, and before we knew it, the party had come to a stop. Just when Prince and Satti were ready to come to blows, Jasleen and Mahi showed up.

Prince's eyes got wide as he stared at Jasleen. Then suddenly, he yelled, "You fuckin' bitch! How could you?"

Jasleen was frozen. The sight of Prince was too much for her to handle.

Harman looked at her and said, "Go back inside, Jasleen." But she couldn't move.

Then Prince yelled out, "I can't believe you hid this from me!"

Harman, and everyone else, was confused. He looked at Prince and said, "What are you talking about?"

"You know exactly what I'm talking about!"

"You're not making any sense bro."

"All you guys know." He pointed at Jasleen and said, "She's pregnant!"

Everyone in the crowd who didn't already know was shocked and began murmuring to each other. But the rest of us were too pre-occupied to care.

Harman said, "Who told you that?"

Prince said, "It don't matter. It's true ain't it?"

"Look, that's none of your business."

"What the fuck you mean it's none of my business? I'm the fuckin' father!"

Harman responded emphatically. "No you're not!" Then he pointed at me and said, "*He* is!"

Until then, I had just been a guy standing there on the side, but now Prince knew who I was. It would have been bad enough if I was Jasleen's new boyfriend — that alone would have set him off. But I was something much worse. I was the guy pretending to be the father of his kid. And when he realized that, he completely lost his mind. He rushed towards me in a murderous rage yelling, "It's *your* kid? It's *your* kid, you piece of shit?" I didn't know what to say or do. I wanted to defend Jasleen, but how do you defend someone from the danger *you* put them in?

There were just enough people in the way to keep Prince from getting to me, but he still tried his hardest to break through. Finally, he gave up, turned to Jasleen and said, "Is that true? Is it his kid?" Not a word out of Jasleen. He kept asking. "Answer me!"

Satti pushed him back. "She don't have to answer nothin! Get the fuck outta here!"

But Prince refused to let up. "I want her to say it! Jasleen,

181

tell me it's not my kid and I'll leave right now."

Finally, Harman looked at Jasleen and said, "Jasleen, just tell'em."

But Jasleen couldn't do that. Suddenly, tears started falling from her eyes, which only added to the confusion. The more Prince pressed her for an answer, the more she cried, and pretty soon… everyone knew the truth. Mahi put her arms around her, and the rest of us couldn't do anything except stand there and watch her break down.

While everyone was trying to wrap their heads around what they had just realized, Mahi started saying Jasleen's name over and over, and each time, more frantically. "Jasleen… Jasleen… Jasleen! *Jasleen!*" All of a sudden, Jasleen's body went limp and Mahi was struggling to hold her up. We all rushed over as Jasleen collapsed to the floor.

Chapter 20 - Hero

By the time we got to the hospital, everyone in the family knew the story. The story about how Jasleen became pregnant with the child of her abusive ex-boyfriend. The story about how she thought her life was over, until this stranger came along and decided to sacrifice his own future just to help her out of this impossible situation. All of a sudden, I was a hero to all of these people... at a time when I never felt like more of a villain.

The sight at the hospital was a trip. So many guests from the party showed up that the place became flooded with fancily dressed Punjabi people. Everywhere you went, from the parking lot to the lobby, you saw men in fancy suits and women in brightly colored saris and lehengas.

Me, Mahi, Harman, Candice, the parents, and Satti's entire family were in the ER waiting room, each going through our own forms of dread. Because of her two miscarriages, Jasleen's Mom was worried the same thing was gonna happen to her daughter. The Aunt had her arm around her, trying, for the first time, to be a sister instead of a sister-in-law. Jasleen's Dad was sitting a few seats away from the rest of us. His tie was loosened and his head was in his hands, as if he had already given up hope. Candice walked over and offered him some water, but he turned it down. Harman kept checking with the nurses for an update, but they couldn't give us one.

Me, I had my own way of dealing with nightmares. Instead of hoping for the best, I would imagine the worst. I would picture as many terrible outcomes as I could, because I felt like if I *thought* of it, it couldn't happen. Normally that worked, but there was nothing about that night that was normal.

Sitting directly across from me was Mahi. I'm sure she was a wreck too, but I couldn't tell. I couldn't bring myself to look at her.

As we were waiting to hear something, some unwelcome guests showed up — Prince, his friends, and his parents, who must have just found out about their future grandchild. Usually, Punjabi parents behave with a certain level of respect towards each other, especially in a situation like this, but these people came into that room without any sense of decency at all. As soon as they spotted Jasleen's parents, they marched over and Prince's Dad yelled in Punjabi, "I hope you're happy!"

We were all taken aback. No introduction, no greeting. Just outrage. He continued, "What kind of people *are* you? Who would do something like this?"

Then Prince's Mom jumped in. Usually moms are the reasonable ones, but this lady was even more angry than her husband. In an ear-splittingly sharp voice, she said, "If anything happens to that baby, we're gonna hold you responsible!"

Jasleen's parents weren't just dealing with their concern for Jasleen and the baby, they were trying to process the shock of finding out the truth about who the father was. All of this was too much for them to handle. Jasleen's Dad was disturbed by the way Prince's parents were acting, but still tried his best to be civil. He said, "Paaji [brother], this isn't the time for all this."

But Prince's Dad wasn't about to let up. He said, "Don't tell me about time! What about all this time you were keeping this secret from us?"

Satti's Dad finally got sick of the insults. He stood up and said, "Shut up and sit down! We don't need this right now!"

Prince's Dad shouted back. "I don't care what you need! What about what *we* need?"

The argument got out of control. The hospital staff tried to calm them down, and when that didn't work, they called security. The two sides were separated and Prince and his people were told sit on the opposite side of the waiting room.

There was still no word about what was going on with Jasleen. At first, we thought she had just become overwhelmed and passed out and that was it. According to Candice, fainting was a common thing during pregnancy, and we all held on to that to make us feel better. But the longer the doctors were taking to tell us anything, the more and more anxious we became. I don't think I had ever prayed in my entire life, but that night, I begged God, *Please, please let this girl and this baby be okay. I've never asked you for anything and I'll never ask you for anything again. I'll do whatever you say and live however you want me to live — just don't let anything happen to them.*

Finally, a nurse came outside and said Jasleen's name. The parents, Harman and Mahi walked up to her, while the rest of us watched and held our breath. I tried my best to read lips and facial expressions, but I couldn't make out what they were saying. Then, Jasleen's Mom started crying. My heart sank. The nurse went back inside, and the family walked back towards the rest of us. Harman looked around at everyone, took a deep breath and said, "They're gonna be okay."

My prayers had been answered. I didn't even think they deserved to be listened to, but someone must have thought otherwise. And I was thankful they did.

I sat there calmly while the family took turns visiting Jasleen. The parents went first, then Harman and Mahi, then Candice and a few other friends. Finally, it was my turn. But just as I was about to walk inside, Prince came over. He looked at Harman and said, "Yo, I'm going next."

Harman said, "I don't think that's a good idea Prince."

"I'm the father of the kid. I have a fuckin' right to go see her."

"Look man, she's been through a lot. Just give her some time."

"What do you think I'm gonna do in there? I'm just gonna see how she's doing and talk to her. That's all."

"Maybe she's not ready to see you."

Prince pointed at me and said, "So the fuckin' fake father gets to see her before the real one does? What kinda bullshit is that?"

Harman said, "She *asked* to see him." Prince didn't like that, but before he could respond, Harman continued, "Look, just hang back for a little while, alright. You'll get to see her. Just give me some time."

Prince finally backed off. "Fine, but I'm not waiting too much longer. And my parents wanna see her too."

Harman said, "Okay, okay... just be patient."

Then Prince stared us both down and said, "And lemme just make some shit real clear. I'm gonna be a part of my kid's life whether y'all like it or not. So you might as well accept that now. Don't try to pull no shit... cause then we're gonna have some real problems."

After he walked away, Harman looked at me and gave me the nod.

When I got into the room, I saw Jasleen lying there, staring off into space. Her body looked drained, but she seemed peaceful in a way. The sound of my footsteps made her turn towards me, but her expression barely changed.

I had never been so ashamed to look into someone's eyes. As carefully as possible, I said, "Hey."

She stared at me for a moment, then gave me a tired smile.

I said, "How are you feeling?"

She said, "I'm okay."

I sat down on a chair next to her bed. The whole time I was in the waiting room, I tried to think of what I would say to her but I couldn't quite figure it out. So I hoped that once I saw her, the words would just come to me. They didn't. I sat there quietly, wondering where to start. Finally, Jasleen broke the silence. She said, "Mahi told me you guys grew up together."

I nodded.

It took a lot of energy for her to speak, but she continued, "I said to her, 'I don't remember seeing him at the wedding.' And she said, 'Yeah, because he wasn't there.' I thought that was kinda weird. And then I asked her if you guys were ever 'together', and she said no. But she hesitated for just a second. And that little hesitation... told me everything. It told me who *she* was to *you*... and who *you* were to *her*."

It took her a *moment* to figure out what it took me a lifetime to. Then she said, "There's only one thing I don't understand. What did you think was gonna happen? How did you think this was all gonna end up?"

I shrugged and said, "I don't know. Not like this."

I wanted her to know how sorry I was, but 'sorry' is the only word that never lives up to its meaning. So I sat there trying to find a better way to say it.

She must have figured out what I was thinking though, because after another moment of silence, she said, "Listen... I don't care why you did what you did. I'm still grateful you did it."

I said, "You sure about that?"

"Yeah, I mean, look at me — I'm in a hospital bed, I'm pregnant, I don't have a man, my family probably hates me, my crazy ex is outside and I have no idea what my future holds — and for some reason, I still have this feeling I'm gonna be okay. And I don't think I would feel like that if it wasn't for you."

There was nothing she could say to make me feel worthy of her gratitude, but I was relieved to know she wasn't broken. The world came crashing down on her that night, and I was worried she wouldn't survive. But when she woke up in that hospital bed, she must have remembered who she was.

I said, "Look, I know I can't do much about most of those things... but you know you still got a man. I mean, don't get me wrong, you deserve much, much better, and so far, I've probably been the strangest kinda man you can think of. But if you'll let me... I promise you, from now on, I'll be as normal as it gets. I'll marry you tomorrow, I swear to god."

She laughed.

I said, "I'm serious."

She said, "You know that's not gonna work."

"Why not?"

"You *know* why not."

I leaned back in my chair and looked up at her heart monitor. I listened to it beep for a while, then looked back at Jasleen. "You remember that night when you told me you were pregnant?"

She nodded.

"You know what I was doing when you asked me to come see you? I was pre-gaming at Lucky's house, getting ready to go out. And I don't know if I ever told you this about me, but I really like going out. I like it more than I like anything. I get to drink, I get to hang out with my boys, have a good time, meet girls. But for some reason, I passed all that up, just to go see *you*. A girl I barely knew. A girl who disappeared on me without saying a word, who had been ignoring my calls and texts for a week. If you were any other girl, I would've just said, 'Hey sorry, I'm kinda busy... maybe some other time.' But I didn't even *think* about saying that, not even for a second. And it wasn't because I didn't want to, it was because I *couldn't*. Because even before all this craziness, even before I had any idea who you were... something about me and you together made sense to me. And after everything we've been through... it still does."

She took a moment to let it all sink in. Then she said, "When I met you... I really liked you too. Like a lot. The way you said things, the way you did things, you were just so... unique. I remember that was the word I used when I described you to my friends. And I remember being excited about what was gonna happen between us, because you're right... there really *was* something about me and you. And there still is. And maybe it's true... maybe we *can* be good together." She paused. "But what's gonna happen every time my brother and his wife come around? Are you ever gonna stop looking at her the way you look at her now? The way you probably have always looked at her?"

I didn't have an answer.

"I know you'll try. But you shouldn't have to try. And I wouldn't want you to. What I want… is someone to look at *me* the way you look at *her*." She paused for a moment to rest her voice. "You know, there was a thing you said to me once that I could never get out of my head. You said that girls always settle for less than they deserve. That really stuck with me, because when I found out I was pregnant, I didn't feel like I deserved *anything*. Except punishment. But you made it sound like that wasn't true. Like it wasn't true at all. And I believed you. And I decided I wasn't gonna settle until I got what I deserved. But if after everything we went through… I settle for being someone's second choice… then what was it all for? What was the point? I know you feel guilty and you're worried about me, and you're thinking 'What's gonna happen to this girl?' and you wanna do something about it. But there's nothing to for you to do, because this girl's gonna be fine… with or without someone."

Then she reached out, put her hand on mine and said, "You did a good thing Indo. Don't ruin it by trying to rescue me."

I looked down at her hand and held on to it for a long while. Then I stood up, leaned over and kissed her on her forehead.

There was a knock on the door. A few moments later, Jasleen's Dad came into the room. In Punjabi, he said, "How are you feeling Jasleen?"

She said, "I'm better."

He nodded. "Someone wanted to see you."

"Who?"

Then he turned around and made a gesture towards the

doorway. Prince's parents walked in.

Jasleen was a little taken aback and understandably wary of them. I got up and moved aside to give them room. They looked like they had calmed down, but I decided to stay in the corner just in case.

Prince's Dad looked down at Jasleen and in Punjabi, said, "How are you dear? We're Prince's Mom and Dad."

Jasleen said, "Sat Sri Akal. I'm... doing better."

He said, "That's good to hear."

Then Prince's Mom smiled and said, "You really scared us, you know."

Jasleen said, "I know. I'm sorry."

The Mom said, "No, no, that's okay. You don't have to be sorry. We're just glad you and the baby are okay. That's all that matters."

There was a long, uneasy silence. Jasleen didn't know what to make of it all. Then Prince's Dad turned to Jasleen's Dad, and in Punjabi said, "Paaji, the truth is... what your daughter did to my son, and to us... it was terrible. I'm not trying to make her feel bad, but there's no other way to say it. We all know that. And most people would never forgive something like that. But she's the mother of our grandchild, so we're willing to move past it. Whatever happened, happened. Let's leave it all behind us and get these two married as soon as possible. No matter how you look at it... we really don't have any other choice."

It all sounded so familiar. Almost the exact same words Harman delivered on his Dad's behalf to me and Jasleen. But Jasleen's Dad wasn't me. This is exactly what he wanted all along. For Jasleen to marry the father of her baby. And even though he wasn't too thrilled about the people he was entering into a union with, it was the best he could hope for.

He sat there for a moment or two, taking it all in. Finally, he looked at Prince's Dad, and in Punjabi said, "Paaji... when I found out my daughter was pregnant, it hurt me so much. You have no idea. I thought, 'Where did I go wrong?' 'How did I let this happen?' But eventually, I accepted it. She's my only daughter after all. And then... tonight, I found out she lied to all of us about who the father of her baby was. I couldn't believe it. That's when I knew that this girl, whoever she was, wasn't the same girl I raised. *That* girl was gone and she was never coming back." Then he paused and took a deep breath. "But after meeting your son, and after meeting you... I breathed a sigh of relief. And I thanked god that she was gone. Because *that* girl, the one that *I* raised... she never would've been strong enough to do what *this* one did. And now that I know why she did it... I don't blame her at all." Then he folded his hands and said, "Thank you for your offer, but our daughter is never going to marry your son."

The look on Jasleen's face when she heard her Dad say those words made me forget every moment that came before it. It made me forget there was ever a struggle to end up where we did. That there was ever even a *time* when things weren't the way they should be.

And the looks on Prince's parents' faces reminded me that some people still had a ways to go. I don't think they had ever dealt with rejection, because it seemed like they were having a hard time processing it. But once they finally did, they turned right back into the hateful creatures they first showed up as. Prince's Dad looked at his wife and in Punjabi, said, "I don't believe this guy." Then he turned back to Jasleen's Dad and said,

"Here we are, trying to help you and your daughter out, and you're turning *us* down? Are you out of your mind?"

Jasleen's Dad didn't respond.

"Look, I'm gonna be nice and give you some more time to think about this. I don't want you to make any stupid decisions."

Jasleen's Dad, very matter-of-factly said, "I don't need any more time... so, if you can please leave us alone now, I want to talk to my daughter," and sat down next to Jasleen.

That's when Prince's Dad lost it. "What the hell *is* this? If I wanted, I could've made you get on your knees and beg me to let your daughter marry my son! But instead I decided to be generous. And this is how you're gonna treat me?! You think you can do that and get away with it?"

He went on and on but Jasleen's Dad took it all in stride. Didn't even react. Until Prince's Dad went too far.

He said, "You just made the biggest mistake of your life! You think anyone else is gonna marry this whore now?"

All of a sudden, Jasleen's Dad looked up at Prince's Dad... then exploded out of his chair and grabbed him by the collar. "What did you say?" Prince's Dad was stunned. It was like a part of Jasleen's Dad that had been dormant for years suddenly reawakened. He went from a dignified, immigrant father to a hot-blooded Punjabi teenager in a village gang fight. The 'hood' in him came out.

He yelled, "Say it again! Say it again!"

It was obvious Prince's Dad was frightened by the rage in Jasleen's Dad's eyes, but he still tried his best to put up a brave front. With shaky confidence, he yelled back, "Oh so this is who you really are, huh?! This is what's underneath all that money?"

I rushed over, jumped in between them and pulled Jasleen's

193

Dad off of him. If I would've got there a second later, I'm convinced he would've broken Prince's Dad's nose. All in the name of defending his daughter.

It was beautiful. Jasleen must have been so proud. I know *I* was.

All the shouting created another scene and security was called again. This time, they got an idea of who was to blame and forced Prince's parents to leave the hospital. Once they were gone, I decided I should leave the room too. I looked at Jasleen and her Dad and said, "Alright... I'll let you guys talk."

Jasleen's Dad said, "Thank you. Thank you for everything son."

The last thing I saw was Jasleen looking at me with tears in her eyes. But they were unlike any other tears I had ever seen her cry.

Over the next hour or so, Harman began encouraging all the friends and relatives to go home. It was almost two in the morning, everyone was tired and there wasn't much left to do. So one by one, they all took off. Once all the relatives were gone, Harman asked Mahi to take the parents home too. She agreed and we all said our goodbyes. The last one to say it was me. After giving the parents hugs, I looked at Mahi and said, "It was good seeing you again."

She took a deep breath and said, "You too."

Only me, Harman, and Satti remained in the waiting room. Even though everyone's primary concern — the well-being of Jasleen and the baby — was alleviated, we still had one major problem on our hands: Prince. Whether Jasleen's family liked it or not, they were stuck with him. Prince was right; he was the father of her kid and that was something nobody could change, no matter how hard they tried. And as long as he was around, he would bring nothing but misery into their lives.

He was still sitting there with a couple of his friends, across the room from us, refusing to budge. Harman wanted to go over and have a talk with him, but Satti wanted to take a more aggressive approach and the two of them started quietly arguing about the best way to go.

While they went back and forth about what to do, all I could think about was where we had ended up. Until that night, Harman, his Dad and Satti were my enemies, and now, we were on the same side. All the resentment I had towards them was gone, and I couldn't get over how suddenly it disappeared. How something I held on to so tightly could let go of *me* so easily.

Sitting across the room from us was a new grudge for me to hold. Someone new for me to hate. But no matter how hard I tried, I couldn't bring myself to. After seeing how fickle hate could be, it didn't seem worth the trouble anymore.

Harman and Satti kept at it for a while but couldn't come to an agreement. Eventually, they decided to go see Jasleen again. And it wasn't too long after that, that I saw Prince reach for his phone, get up, and walk towards the exit, alone. I stood up and followed.

When I got outside, he was standing in front of the building, on a call with someone. So, I leaned against a column, put my hands in my pockets and waited for him to finish. Finally, he hung up and turned around. The sight of me instantly brought back all of the rage.

He said, "Why you still here, bruh? Why don't you go home?"

I said, "I will... sooner or later."

He said, "Good." Then he looked around to see if anyone was there and said, "And you better watch your back from now on homie. Don't think I'm gonna forget about what you did."

I looked at him, confused. "And what did I do?"

"You serious? You don't remember tryin' to steal my kid from me?"

"You mean, *my* kid."

"Excuse me?" He got in my face. "That shit's already over bro."

"You sure about that? Did they do a DNA test I don't know about?"

"I don't need no fuckin' DNA test. Me and Jasleen fucked before we broke up. And then she got pregnant. That's all the proof I need."

"How you know she didn't fuck anybody else?"

He didn't like the idea of that at all. He said, "Cause Jasleen ain't that typa girl."

I let out a laugh. "Really? We're talking about the same Jasleen, right?"

I felt his heart sink just a little. He stuck his finger in my chest and said, "You got something you trying to say? Spit it out bitch!"

"Well I'm just trying to make sure we're talking about the same girl. Cause the one *I* met, she had just barely broken up with her boyfriend... and two days later, she was in the backseat of my car."

He didn't wanna believe it. But he couldn't help himself. Then I stared into his eyes and said, "And from what I remember... we did more than enough to make a baby."

Sometimes it takes a lie to make the truth come out. He swung as hard as he could and hit me in the jaw.

It hurt. Real bad. But it wasn't as bad as watching Jasleen collapse to the floor. Or being in the waiting room, terrified that her and the baby weren't gonna make it.

The force of the punch dropped me to my knees and blurred my vision for a moment. When I was finally able to see straight, I looked up at him and said, "Was that how you hit Jasleen?"

He shouted, "Fuck you motherfucker!" and swung again. This time he got me in the side of the head and I went to the ground. He stood towering over me and said, "Whose kid is it?"

With as much of a voice as I could muster up, I said, "You asking me or yourself?"

He kicked me in the ribs. "Answer the fuckin question! Whose kid is it?"

I looked up at him and said, "Jasleen's."

He asked me the same question… over and over. And I gave him the same answer… over and over. The last thing I remember was hearing voices screaming at him to stop. God knows who they belonged to.

Chapter 21 – Maybe Even Worse

When I found out Mahi got into Stanford, I wasn't happy. Because I knew things between us were never gonna be the same. She would be spending more and more of her time with all these smart, 'college-type' people, and less and less time with me, and eventually, she'd outgrow our relationship. So, before she could do that to me, I decided to do something to her. That's why I went to Chico. To show her that I didn't need her, because I was afraid that someday, *she* wouldn't need *me*.

I did the same thing when I found out she had a boyfriend. I was hurt, but instead of admitting it, I decided I was gonna act like I didn't care. I thought, 'How could she move on without me?' 'How could she forget about me so easily?' Never mind the fact that I did all kinds of things with all kinds of girls while I was away at college. That didn't matter. In my mind, she betrayed me and she had to be punished.

The day we saw each other again after I got back from Chico, I was expecting her to be a different person. I thought she would talk differently and act differently and be nothing close to the girl I remembered. But as soon as we looked into each other's eyes, I knew she was exactly the same. Whatever was between us before, was still there and I turned out to be completely wrong. She hadn't moved on and she hadn't forgotten about me. It was still in my hands to make me and her a thing... but I chose not to.

You know, there are these guys like Prince who get jealous and try to control their girlfriends, and they do crazy, destructive things. But at least they're somewhat honest about how they feel. At least they reveal something about themselves, instead of trying to keep it all hidden like I always did.

Mahi meant everything to me. Since the very first time I saw her. Since the day my Dad carried me to her house in the rain without an umbrella and asked her Mom to watch me. I was four years old and Mahi's family had just moved into the neighborhood a few months earlier. My parents had never spoken to them, but they looked like us and I guess that was enough. My Mom was working overtime that day, and my Dad was getting late for work, so he explained the situation to Mahi's Mom and said, "Can you watch my son until my wife comes home?"

She smiled and said, "Of course."

She took me into the living room, sat me down on the couch and left. And now I was in this strange house by myself, terrified. But then... in walked this angelic little girl with surma in her eyes, carrying a folded towel. I couldn't take my eyes off of her. We stared at each other for a moment, then she handed me the towel and in Punjabi said, "This is for the rain on you" as if she was trying to repeat something she was told to say. Then she ran away.

Life starts out so big and complicated. There are so many directions a guy can go and so many feelings he can feel that it's impossible not to be overwhelmed. But somewhere along the way, we'll all have that moment when we look into the wrong pair of eyes and suddenly understand how simple this whole thing really is. That when it comes down to it, it's nothing more than me and a girl. And even if the girl changes a thousand times, the story never does.

I might have only been four years old, but when that little girl walked into that room, I knew two things: that I needed her, and I needed her to need *me*. That was the truth. That was the truest truth. And anytime I was threatened, I covered up that truth with the biggest lie I could tell. That Mahi meant nothing to me. That was my way of hurting her. And I did it over and over.

We might do it in different ways, but we'll all hurt the girls we know… that much is for sure. That's what we've been doing since the beginning of time. Because we figured out early on that they have the power to hurt *us* a thousand times worse than any other man can. You can recover from anything a *man* can do to you, but a *woman* can leave you permanently damaged. And all our attempts to harm them, control them, or keep them down are a reaction to that knowledge.

Here I was, thinking I was different, thinking I was one of the good guys, fighting for Raveena, fighting for Jasleen, fighting for every girl I knew and every girl I didn't. But it turned out, I was just like all the guys I always talked shit about. Maybe even worse.

Chapter 22 – Yours To Keep

I woke up in an empty hospital room with vague memories of the night before — a nurse cleaning blood off my face, a doctor giving me concussion tests, a police officer taking my statement. As I laid there, trying to piece everything together, Harman and Satti walked in and filled in all the blanks.

Prince had gotten arrested, and to no one's surprise, he was already on probation. And since the 'fight' was caught on surveillance cameras, it looked like he was going away for a while. Obviously, it wouldn't be forever, but at least Jasleen could raise her kid in peace for a few years. I asked them how she was doing, and Harman said, "She's better. We took her home a little while ago."

I said, "Oh... that's good."

"Yeah, she came and sat with you for a bit. You were asleep."

The way he was talking, it seemed like Jasleen had told them about me and her. But he didn't mention it. Instead, he gave me a long look, shook his head and said, "Who *are* you bro?"

The answer to that question was a lot more complicated than he thought it was. Then he said, "Thank you for everything you did man, seriously. My family's forever in debt to you. We

might even have to put up a picture of you in our living room."
I laughed.

After they left, a nurse came in for one last check up and said
I'd be discharged in an hour or so. Then I was left alone again. I
was sore in a lot of places, had a bad headache, and it hurt to
breathe... but I felt cleansed. Like my sins had been washed
away.

At some point I must have fallen back asleep, because a
knock on the door woke me up. I didn't have enough energy to
say, 'Come in', so I just waited. A moment later, Mahi walked
into the room.

She winced when she saw my face. I said, "Don't worry, it
looks worse than it feels."

She sat down on a chair next to the bed. Her eyes looked
tired and her body seemed worn out. I guess everyone who
went through the night before had something to show for it. She
said, "How are you?"

I said, "I'm okay."

There was a short silence, then she shook her head and said,
"What happened last night?"

I shrugged. "I don't know."

"It feels like a bad dream."

"Yeah. But at least we got to wake up from it."

It had been a while since Harman and Satti left my room, so
I asked, "Is Harman still here?"

She said, "No... he's home. I came alone."

"Oh."

She nodded.

There was another short silence. Then I said, "You know, I
tried real hard to hate that fucker... but he doesn't make it easy."

She laughed. "You know what's funny? When I first met him, I tried to hate him too... but I couldn't do it either."

"Really?"

"Yeah. He was like this way too perfect guy. It was super annoying."

I laughed. "Annoying why?"

"I don't know... I mean, it wasn't really him, I guess it was more just me. I was... just in a weird place at the time."

"What do you mean?"

"Nothing... it's a long story."

I shrugged and said, "Well, I got some time to kill, so..."

She thought about it for a long moment. Finally, she said, "When I first started going to Stanford, I hated it. I didn't feel like I was good enough to be there. Like they made some huge mistake and accidentally let me in. And the people there were so different than the people in high school. Not in a bad way — just different, you know. I didn't fit in with them at all. And what made everything worse was that *you* were gone. Because with you, I always had a place I belonged.

"Anyway, by the end of my first semester I was seriously considering dropping out. And that's when I met Harman. And he was like I said — that perfect guy you see in movies. Handsome and charming, always had his hair perfectly combed, no wrinkles in his clothes, all that stuff. As much as I felt like a misfit in that place, he was the total opposite. He looked like he was at home there. And he just kinda got on my nerves. I guess also because he was Punjabi too, and he had sorta figured this whole thing out and I was still struggling — I don't know. But then, as I got to know him, I realized he was a genuinely good person. And then he started liking me. Like, 'liking me' liking me. And when that happened, it kinda felt like… that whole *place* started liking me too. And he took me from hating it there to loving it.

"It felt good for a while, having a boyfriend for the first time and all that… but the more serious our relationship became, the more I started to freak out. Because in the back of my mind, I always saw myself ending up with you. That was, you know, going back to when we were kids. You remember when your uncles and aunts used to joke that me and you were gonna get married someday? That wasn't a joke to me, that was just… what was gonna happen. What I wanted to happen. So now, I was in a situation where I didn't know what to do, because it wasn't like I knew how *you* felt about *me*. What if that was just some one-sided, childhood fantasy, and Harman was the one I actually belonged with? I had no idea. And every day I felt more lost and more confused and more guilty.

"And then I found out Harman was getting ready to propose to me. I guess he asked my parents for permission or something, and you know them, they can't keep secrets. It wasn't like they told me or anything, but they started acting all weird and dropping hints and stuff and so I figured it out. And now everything was much, much worse.

"Somewhere around that time, I found out you were coming back. And I was like, 'Okay, finally I'll get my answer.' The day I was supposed to come see you, I tried my best to not have any expectations… but I couldn't help it. It sounds kinda stupid, but I actually pictured exactly how the whole thing was gonna go. Like after we talked for a while, I was gonna say, 'Guess what? I got a boyfriend now.' And you were gonna be surprised but act like you didn't care, because… of course. But I would see through it. And then I was gonna tell you that Harman was getting ready to propose to me and ask you what I should do. And you would say, 'I don't know, it's up to you.' And I'd say, 'Would you be okay with it if I said yes?' And you'd say, 'Why wouldn't I be?' And I'd keep trying to get an answer out of you and you'd keep giving me nothing. And finally, I would get upset and start to leave, and just as I was about to walk out the door, you would stop me… and tell me what I'd been waiting to hear my whole life.

"Like I said, I know it sounds stupid, but that's what I really thought was gonna happen. But it didn't happen like that at all.

"When I went home that night, it was like the end of the world. Something I believed in so strongly, for so long, turned out to not be real. And I had to ask myself, 'Is there something wrong with me?' 'Am I crazy?'

"That's why on my wedding day, when they told me you were sick, I hoped you were faking it. Because I just needed to know I wasn't crazy. Because if you would've shown up, I would've spent the rest of my life believing that I was. But when I found out you weren't coming, just for that moment, it gave me hope. Not for us to end up together — it was already too late for that. Just hope that you felt about *me* the way I felt about *you.* I wanted that more than anything. And that little bit of hope helped me get over everything I had to get over.

"But you know, even though I'm good now and I'm really happy with my life… every once in a while, when I'm by myself, waiting for Harman to come home… I remember back to when we used to play house. And just for a moment, I wonder what it would be like if instead of him… *you* walked through the door. Like how that would feel, and what you would say to me, and what I would say to you…"

205

As she continued describing the life we could have had, I felt something I hadn't felt since I was a kid... tears in my eyes. Mahi wasn't looking directly at me, so I tried my hardest to will the tears back to wherever they were coming from. But I couldn't. There were too many. Then one of them rolled down my face. And then another one, and then another. Finally, Mahi looked up.

My whole life, I tried to give her as little of me as possible, and now, all of a sudden, she was staring at all of it. She was overwhelmed — like she was feeling every feeling all at once. All the good ones and all the bad ones. I was trying my hardest to hold my self together, but then, she put her arms around me, as if to say it was okay to let go. So I did.

I always knew I was carrying something heavy around. I could feel it everywhere I went. But it wasn't until it all came out that I realized just how much harm it was doing to me. Those tears, when you hold on to them, they're like poison. A poison that separates you from the rest of the world. And it's only when you let them go, that you can become one with anything other than yourself.

When there was nothing left to let go, I looked at Mahi, much differently than I had ever looked at her before. But I didn't have any words that I thought could do her any good. What I did to her was unforgiveable, and there was nothing I could say to make up for it. The only thing I could do was try. I said, "I'm glad you're doing good. I really am. For the longest time, I was hoping you were miserable like me, but not anymore. Now I just want you to be happy, and stay happy... cause that's what you deserve. And as long as you get what you deserve, I'll be okay with getting what *I* deserve."

She listened… then wiped the remaining tears off my face and said, "If *you* get to decide what *I* deserve… can *I* decide what *you* deserve?"

I didn't say anything.

She continued, "Look, I can tell you all this happened because it was meant to happen, and there was nothing either of us could've done to stop it, cause that really is the truth. But I know you're not gonna believe me. So if you feel like you owe me something… then I'll ask you for something. Forgive yourself for whatever you think you did."

I took a deep breath and said, "Can you ask for something else?"

She shook her head. "There's nothing else I want."

She paused for a moment, then said, "And there's something else I want you to know. I love my husband. I'm gonna have kids with him, I'm gonna grow old with him, and I'm gonna die with him. But I wasn't *made* for him. I was made for you.

"Most people never even *find* the person they're made for… but *I* got to spend the first 18 years of my life with him. And for that, the only thing I can be is grateful."

I always thought I lost what we had. But hearing those words made me realize that once you're given something like that, it's yours to keep. The only thing that changes is what it makes you feel. Sometimes it's joy, sometimes it's pain, but in the end it's all the same, and you should appreciate it the same. Mahi wasn't coming back to me, but as long as it hurt to be apart, I knew we'd always be together.

She got up to get me some tissues, but all she could find were some paper towels. She handed them over and as I cleaned myself up, I said, "You probably think I'm a bitch now… seeing me cry."

She said, "Nah… I *already* thought you were a bitch."

I smiled and said, "Okay good. Then I got nothing to worry about."

She smiled back.

It felt like she was getting ready to go, so I said, "You wanna chill for a while?"

She said "Okay," then started looking around to find a place to sit. I moved over to make some room on the bed and she sat down next to me. All the words had already been said; the only thing left for us to do now was enjoy each other's company one last time. So that's what we did. And as we sat there in that beautiful silence, she put her head on my shoulder.

And it's been there ever since.

ABOUT THE AUTHOR

Born and raised in Northern California, Ik Jagait is an independent writer and filmmaker. Influenced by stories of his grandmother, who struggled through a subjugated life in rural Punjab and passed away before he was born, much of his work centers around the theme of female oppression.

www.IkJagait.com
Instagram @ikjagait

Made in the USA
Monee, IL
25 November 2021

83004294R00132